HERBERT WEST:
REANIMATOR

AND OTHER TALES

HERBERT WEST: REANIMATOR

AND OTHER TALES

H.P. LOVECRAFT

THIS EDITION was adapted from various print and digital story versions in the public domain. It maintains the unabridged content and spelling of the original magazine publications, though some minimal punctuation and diacritical usage has been modernized.

Published for the Supernatural Fox Sisters' Supernatural History Series—collections of books and artifact reproductions focusing on places and events in supernatural history.

Cover image: *Dissection of a green frog.* Engraving by August Johann Rösel von Rosenhof. Figure XVI of *Historia naturalis ranarum nostratium in qua omnes earum proprietates, praesertim quae ad generationem ipsarum pertinent, fusius enarrantur* (1758). from the American Museum of Natural History.

Front cover designed by Omar Rodriguez Rodriguez.

Typesetting, editing & back-cover text by Katie Fox.

Frontispiece adapted from illustration for "Herbert West: Reanimator" in the November 1942 issue of *Weird Tales*. Artist: Damon Knight.

ISBN: 978-1-947587-04-5

First trade paperback edition

Copyright 2018 by
Katie Fox
San Francisco, Ca.

All rights reserved.

FOXEDITING.COM

CONTENTS

That is not dead which can eternal lie.

And with strange aeons even death may die.

—Abdul Alhazred, *The Necronomicon*

Herbert West: Reanimator

I. From the Dark

OF Herbert West, who was my friend in college and in after life, I can speak only with extreme terror. This terror is not due altogether to the sinister manner of his recent disappearance, but was engendered by the whole nature of his life-work, and first gained its acute form more than seventeen years ago, when we were in the third year of our course at the Miskatonic University Medical School in Arkham. While he was with me, the wonder and diabolism of his experiments fascinated me utterly, and I was his closest companion. Now that he is gone and the spell is broken, the actual fear is greater. Memories and possibilities are ever more hideous than realities.

The first horrible incident of our acquaintance was the greatest shock I ever experienced, and it is only with reluctance that I repeat it. As I have said, it happened when we were in the medical school, where West had already made himself notorious through his wild theories on the nature of death and the possibility of overcoming it artificially. His views, which were widely ridiculed by the faculty and his fellow-students, hinged on the essentially mechanistic nature of life; and concerned means for operating the organic machinery of mankind by calculated chemical action after the failure of natural processes. In his experiments with various animating solutions he had killed and treated immense numbers of rabbits, guinea-pigs, cats, dogs, and monkeys, till he had become the prime nuisance of the college. Several times he had actually obtained signs of life in animals supposedly dead; in many cases violent signs; but he soon saw that the perfection of this process, if indeed possible, would necessarily involve a lifetime of research. It likewise became clear that, since the same solution never worked alike on different organic species, he would require human subjects for further and more specialised progress. It was here that he first came into conflict with the college authorities, and was debarred from future experiments by no less a dignitary than the dean of the medical school himself—the learned and benevolent Dr. Allan Halsey, whose work in behalf of the stricken is recalled by every old resident of Arkham.

I had always been exceptionally tolerant of West's pursuits, and we frequently discussed his theories, whose ramifications and corollaries were almost infinite. Holding with Haeckel that all life is a chemical and physical process, and that the so-called "soul" is a myth, my friend believed that artificial reanimation of the dead can depend only on the condition of the tissues; and that unless actual decomposition has set in, a corpse fully equipped with organs may with suitable measures be set going again in the peculiar fashion known as life. That the psychic or intellectual life might be impaired by the slight deterioration of sensitive brain-cells which even a short period of death would be apt to cause, West fully realised. It had at first been his hope to find a reagent which would restore vitality before the actual advent of death, and only repeated failures on animals had shewn him that the natural and artificial life-motions were incompatible. He then sought extreme freshness in his specimens, injecting his solutions into the blood immediately after the extinction of life. It was this circumstance which made the professors so carelessly sceptical, for they felt that true death had not occurred in any case. They did not stop to view the matter closely and reasoningly.

It was not long after the faculty had interdicted his work that West confided to me his resolution to get fresh human bodies in some manner, and continue in secret the experiments he could no longer perform openly. To hear him discussing ways and means was rather ghastly, for at the college we had never procured anatomical specimens ourselves. Whenever the morgue proved inadequate, two local negroes attended to this matter, and they were seldom questioned. West was then a small, slender, spectacled youth with delicate features, yellow hair, pale blue eyes, and a soft voice, and it was uncanny to hear him dwelling on the relative merits of Christchurch Cemetery and the potter's field. We finally decided on the potter's field, because practically every body in Christchurch was embalmed; a thing of course ruinous to West's researches.

I was by this time his active and enthralled assistant, and helped him make all his decisions, not only concerning the source of bodies but concerning a suitable place for our loathsome work. It was I who thought of the deserted Chapman farmhouse beyond Meadow Hill, where we fitted up on the ground floor an operating room and a laboratory, each with dark curtains to conceal our midnight doings. The place was far from any road, and in sight of no other house, yet precautions were none the less necessary; since rumours of strange lights, started by chance nocturnal roamers, would soon bring disaster on our enterprise. It was agreed to call the whole thing a chemical laboratory if discovery should occur. Gradually we equipped our sinister haunt of science with materials either purchased in Boston or quietly borrowed from the college—materials carefully made unrecognisable save to expert eyes—and provided spades and picks for the many burials we should have to make in the cellar. At the college we used an incinerator, but the apparatus was too costly for our unauthorised laboratory. Bodies were always a nuisance—even the small guinea-pig bodies from the slight clandestine experiments in West's room at the boarding-house.

We followed the local death-notices like ghouls, for our specimens demanded particular qualities. What we wanted were corpses interred soon after death and without artificial preservation; preferably free from malforming disease, and certainly with all organs present. Accident victims were our best hope. Not for many weeks did we hear of anything suitable; though we talked with morgue and hospital authorities, ostensibly in the college's interest, as often as we could without exciting suspicion. We found that the college had first choice in every case, so that it might be necessary to remain in Arkham during the summer, when only the limited summer-school classes were held. In the end, though, luck favoured us; for one day we heard of an almost ideal case in the potter's field; a brawny young workman drowned only the morning before in Sumner's Pond, and buried at the town's expense without delay or embalming. That afternoon we found the new grave, and determined to begin work soon after midnight.

It was a repulsive task that we undertook in the black small hours, even though we lacked at that time the special horror of graveyards which later experiences brought to us. We carried spades and oil dark lanterns, for although electric torches were then manufactured, they were not as satisfactory as the tungsten contrivances of today. The process of unearthing was slow and sordid—it might have been gruesomely poetical if we had been artists instead of scientists—and we were glad when our spades struck wood. When the pine box was fully uncovered West scrambled down and removed the lid, dragging out and propping up the contents. I reached down and hauled the contents out of the grave, and then both toiled hard to restore the spot to its former appearance. The affair made us rather nervous, especially the stiff form and vacant face of our first trophy, but we managed to remove all traces of our visit. When we had patted down the last shovelful of earth we put the specimen in a canvas sack and set out for the old Chapman place beyond Meadow Hill.

On an improvised dissecting-table in the old farmhouse, by the light of a powerful acetylene lamp, the specimen was not very spectral looking. It had been a sturdy and apparently unimaginative youth of wholesome plebeian type—large-framed, grey-eyed, and brown-haired—a sound animal without psychological subtleties, and probably having vital processes of the simplest and healthiest sort. Now, with the eyes closed, it looked more asleep than dead; though the expert test of my friend soon left no doubt on that score. We had at last what West had always longed for—a real dead man of the ideal kind, ready for the solution as prepared according to the most careful calculations and theories for human use. The tension on our part became very great. We knew that there was scarcely a chance for anything like complete success, and could not avoid hideous fears at possible grotesque results of partial animation. Especially were we apprehensive concerning the mind and impulses of the creature, since in the space following death some of the more delicate cerebral cells might well have suffered deterioration. I, myself, still held some curious notions about the traditional "soul" of man, and felt an awe at the secrets that might be told by one returning from the dead. I wondered what sights this placid youth might have seen in inaccessible spheres, and what he could relate if fully restored to life. But my wonder was not overwhelming, since for the most part I shared the materialism of my friend. He was calmer than I as he forced a large quantity of his fluid into a vein of the body's arm, immediately binding the incision securely.

The waiting was gruesome, but West never faltered. Every now and then he applied his stethoscope to the specimen, and bore the negative results philosophically. After about three-quarters of an hour without the least sign of life he disappointedly pronounced the solution inadequate, but determined to make the most of his opportunity and try one change in the formula before disposing of his ghastly prize. We had that afternoon dug a grave in the cellar, and would have to fill it by dawn—for although we had fixed a lock on the house we wished to shun even the remotest risk of a ghoulish discovery. Besides, the body would not be even approximately fresh the next night. So taking the solitary acetylene lamp into the adjacent laboratory, we left our silent guest on the slab in the dark, and bent every energy to the mixing of a new solution; the weighing and measuring supervised by West with an almost fanatical care.

The awful event was very sudden, and wholly unexpected. I was pouring something from one test-tube to another, and West was busy over the alcohol blast-lamp which had to answer for a Bunsen burner in this gasless edifice, when from the pitch-black room we had left there burst the most appalling and daemoniac succession of cries that either of us had ever heard. Not more unutterable could have been the chaos of hellish sound if the pit itself had opened to release the agony of the damned, for in one inconceivable cacophony was centred all the supernal terror and unnatural despair of animate nature. Human it could not have been—it is not in man to make such sounds—and without a thought of our late employment or its possible discovery both West and I leaped to the nearest window like stricken animals; overturning tubes, lamp, and retorts, and vaulting madly into the starred abyss of the rural night. I think we screamed ourselves as we stumbled frantically toward the town, though as we reached the outskirts we put on a semblance of restraint—just enough to seem like belated revellers staggering home from a debauch.

We did not separate, but managed to get to West's room, where we whispered with the gas up until dawn. By then we had calmed ourselves a little with rational theories and plans for investigation, so that we could sleep through the day—classes being disregarded. But that evening two items in the paper, wholly unrelated, made it again impossible for us to sleep. The old deserted Chapman house had inexplicably burned to an amorphous heap of ashes; that we could understand because of the upset lamp. Also, an attempt had been made to disturb a new grave in the potter's field, as if by futile and spadeless clawing at the earth. That we could not understand, for we had patted down the mould very carefully.

And for seventeen years after that West would look frequently over his shoulder, and complain of fancied footsteps behind him. Now he has disappeared.

II. The Plague-Daemon

I shall never forget that hideous summer sixteen years ago, when like a noxious afrite from the halls of Eblis typhoid stalked leeringly through Arkham. It is by that satanic scourge that most recall the year, for truly terror brooded with bat-wings over the piles of coffins in the tombs of Christchurch Cemetery; yet for me there is a greater horror in that time—a horror known to me alone now that Herbert West has disappeared.

West and I were doing post-graduate work in summer classes at the medical school of Miskatonic University, and my friend had attained a wide notoriety because of his experiments leading toward the revivification of the dead. After the scientific slaughter of uncounted small animals the freakish work had ostensibly stopped by order of our sceptical dean, Dr. Allan Halsey; though West had continued to perform certain secret tests in his dingy boarding-house room, and had on one terrible and unforgettable occasion taken a human body from its grave in the potter's field to a deserted farmhouse beyond Meadow Hill.

I was with him on that odious occasion, and saw him inject into the still veins the elixir which he thought would to some extent restore life's chemical and physical processes. It had ended horribly—in a delirium of fear which we gradually came to attribute to our own overwrought nerves—and West had never afterward been able to shake off a maddening sensation of being haunted and hunted. The body had not been quite fresh enough; it is obvious that to restore normal mental attributes a body must be very fresh indeed; and a burning of the old house had prevented us from burying the thing. It would have been better if we could have known it was underground.

After that experience West had dropped his researches for some time; but as the zeal of the born scientist slowly returned, he again became importunate with the college faculty, pleading for the use of the dissecting-room and of fresh human specimens for the work he regarded as so overwhelmingly important. His pleas, however, were wholly in vain; for the decision of Dr. Halsey was inflexible, and the other professors all endorsed the verdict of their leader. In the radical theory of reanimation they saw nothing but the immature vagaries of a youthful enthusiast whose slight form, yellow hair, spectacled blue eyes, and soft voice gave no hint of the supernormal—almost diabolical—power of the cold brain within. I can see him now as he was then—and I shiver. He grew sterner of face, but never elderly. And now Sefton Asylum has had the mishap and West has vanished.

West clashed disagreeably with Dr. Halsey near the end of our last undergraduate term in a wordy dispute that did less credit to him than to the kindly dean in point of courtesy. He felt that he was needlessly and irrationally retarded in a supremely great work; a work which he could of course conduct to suit himself in later years, but which he wished to begin while still possessed of the exceptional facilities of the university. That the tradition-bound elders should ignore his singular results on animals, and persist in their denial of the possibility of reanimation, was inexpressibly disgusting and almost incomprehensible to a youth of West's logical temperament. Only greater maturity could help him understand the chronic mental limitations of the "professor-doctor" type—the product of generations of pathetic Puritanism; kindly, conscientious, and sometimes gentle and amiable, yet always narrow, intolerant, custom-ridden, and lacking in perspective. Age has more charity for these incomplete yet high-souled characters, whose worst real vice is timidity, and who are ultimately punished by general ridicule for their intellectual sins—sins like Ptolemaism, Calvinism, anti-Darwinism, anti-Nietzscheism, and every sort of Sabbatarianism and sumptuary legislation. West, young despite his marvellous scientific acquirements, had scant patience with good Dr. Halsey and his erudite colleagues; and nursed an increasing resentment, coupled with a desire to prove his theories to these obtuse worthies in some striking and dramatic fashion. Like most youths, he indulged in elaborate day-dreams of revenge, triumph, and final magnanimous forgiveness.

And then had come the scourge, grinning and lethal, from the nightmare caverns of Tartarus. West and I had graduated about the time of its beginning, but had remained for additional work at the summer school, so that we were in Arkham when it broke with full daemoniac fury upon the town. Though not as yet licensed physicians, we now had our degrees, and were pressed frantically into public service as the numbers of the stricken grew. The situation was almost past management, and deaths ensued too frequently for the local undertakers fully to handle. Burials without embalming were made in rapid succession, and even the Christchurch Cemetery receiving tomb was crammed with coffins of the unembalmed dead. This circumstance was not without effect on West, who thought often of the irony of the situation—so many fresh specimens, yet none for his persecuted researches! We were frightfully overworked, and the terrific mental and nervous strain made my friend brood morbidly.

But West's gentle enemies were no less harassed with prostrating duties. College had all but closed, and every doctor of the medical faculty was helping to fight the typhoid plague. Dr. Halsey in particular had distinguished himself in sacrificing service, applying his extreme skill with whole-hearted energy to cases which many others shunned because of danger or apparent hopelessness. Before a month was over the fearless dean had become a popular hero, though he seemed unconscious of his fame as he struggled to keep from collapsing with physical fatigue and nervous exhaustion. West could not withhold admiration for the fortitude of his foe, but because of this was even more determined to prove to him the truth of his amazing doctrines. Taking advantage of the disorganisation of both college work and municipal health regulations, he managed to get a recently deceased body smuggled into the university dissecting-room one night, and in my presence injected a new modification of his solution. The thing actually opened its eyes, but only stared at the ceiling with a look of soul-petrifying horror before collapsing into an inertness from which nothing could rouse it. West said it was not fresh enough—the hot summer air does not favour corpses. That time we were almost caught before we incinerated the thing, and West doubted the advisability of repeating his daring misuse of the college laboratory.

The peak of the epidemic was reached in August. West and I were almost dead, and Dr. Halsey did die on the 14th. The students all attended the hasty funeral on the 15th, and bought an impressive wreath, though the latter was quite overshadowed by the tributes sent by wealthy Arkham citizens and by the municipality itself. It was almost a public affair, for the dean had surely been a public benefactor. After the entombment we were all somewhat depressed, and spent the afternoon at the bar of the Commercial House; where West, though shaken by the death of his chief opponent, chilled the rest of us with references to his notorious theories. Most of the students went home, or to various duties, as the evening advanced; but West persuaded me to aid him in "making a night of it." West's landlady saw us arrive at his room about two in the morning, with a third man between us; and told her husband that we had all evidently dined and wined rather well.

Apparently this acidulous matron was right; for about 3 a.m. the whole house was aroused by cries coming from West's room, where when they broke down the door they found the two of us unconscious on the blood-stained carpet, beaten, scratched, and mauled, and with the broken remnants of West's bottles and instruments around us. Only an open window told what had become of our assailant, and many wondered how he himself had fared after the terrific leap from the second story to the lawn which he must have made. There were some strange garments in the room, but West upon regaining consciousness said they did not belong to the stranger, but were specimens collected for bacteriological analysis in the course of investigations on the transmission of germ diseases. He ordered them burnt as soon as possible in the capacious fireplace. To the police we both declared ignorance of our late companion's identity. He was, West nervously said, a congenial stranger whom we had met at some downtown bar of uncertain location. We had all been rather jovial, and West and I did not wish to have our pugnacious companion hunted down.

That same night saw the beginning of the second Arkham horror—the horror that to me eclipsed the plague itself. Christchurch Cemetery was the scene of a terrible killing; a watchman having been clawed to death in a manner not only too hideous for description, but raising a doubt as to the human agency of the deed. The victim had been seen alive considerably after midnight—the dawn revealed the unutterable thing. The manager of a circus at the neighbouring town of Bolton was questioned, but he swore that no beast had at any time escaped from its cage. Those who found the body noted a trail of blood leading to the receiving tomb, where a small pool of red lay on the concrete just outside the gate. A fainter trail led away toward the woods, but it soon gave out.

The next night devils danced on the roofs of Arkham, and unnatural madness howled in the wind. Through the fevered town had crept a curse which some said was greater than the plague, and which some whispered was the embodied daemon-soul of the plague itself. Eight houses were entered by a nameless thing which strewed red death in its wake—in all, seventeen maimed and shapeless remnants of bodies were left behind by the voiceless, sadistic monster that crept abroad. A few persons had half seen it in the dark, and said it was white and like a malformed ape or anthropomorphic fiend. It had not left behind quite all that it had attacked, for sometimes it had been hungry. The number it had killed was fourteen; three of the bodies had been in stricken homes and had not been alive.

On the third night frantic bands of searchers, led by the police, captured it in a house on Crane Street near the Miskatonic campus. They had organised the quest with care, keeping in touch by means of volunteer telephone stations, and when someone in the college district had reported hearing a scratching at a shuttered window, the net was quickly spread. On account of the general alarm and precautions, there were only two more victims, and the capture was effected without major casualties. The thing was finally stopped by a bullet, though not a fatal one, and was rushed to the local hospital amidst universal excitement and loathing.

For it had been a man. This much was clear despite the nauseous eyes, the voiceless simianism, and the daemoniac savagery. They dressed its wound and carted it to the asylum at Sefton, where it beat its head against the walls of a padded cell for sixteen years—until the recent mishap, when it escaped under circumstances that few like to mention. What had most disgusted the searchers of Arkham was the thing they noticed when the monster's face was cleaned—the mocking, unbelievable resemblance to a learned and self-sacrificing martyr who had been entombed but three days before—the late Dr. Allan Halsey, public benefactor and dean of the medical school of Miskatonic University.

To the vanished Herbert West and to me the disgust and horror were supreme. I shudder tonight as I think of it; shudder even more than I did that morning when West muttered through his bandages,

"Damn it, it wasn't *quite* fresh enough!"

III. Six Shots by Midnight

It is uncommon to fire all six shots of a revolver with great suddenness when one would probably be sufficient, but many things in the life of Herbert West were uncommon. It is, for instance, not often that a young physician leaving college is obliged to conceal the principles which guide his selection of a home and office, yet that was the case with Herbert West. When he and I obtained our degrees at the medical school of Miskatonic University, and sought to relieve our poverty by setting up as general practitioners, we took great care not to say that we chose our house because it was fairly well isolated, and as near as possible to the potter's field.

Reticence such as this is seldom without a cause, nor indeed was ours; for our requirements were those resulting from a life-work distinctly unpopular. Outwardly we were doctors only, but beneath the surface were aims of far greater and more terrible moment—for the essence of Herbert West's existence was a quest amid black and forbidden realms of the unknown, in which he hoped to uncover the secret of life and restore to perpetual animation the graveyard's cold clay. Such a quest demands strange materials, among them fresh human bodies; and in order to keep supplied with these indispensable things one must live quietly and not far from a place of informal interment.

West and I had met in college, and I had been the only one to sympathise with his hideous experiments. Gradually I had come to be his inseparable assistant, and now that we were out of college we had to keep together. It was not easy to find a good opening for two doctors in company, but finally the influence of the university secured us a practice in Bolton—a factory town near Arkham, the seat of the college. The Bolton Worsted Mills are the largest in the Miskatonic

Valley, and their polyglot employees are never popular as patients with the local physicians. We chose our house with the greatest care, seizing at last on a rather run-down cottage near the end of Pond Street; five numbers from the closest neighbour, and separated from the local potter's field by only a stretch of meadow land, bisected by a narrow neck of the rather dense forest which lies to the north. The distance was greater than we wished, but we could get no nearer house without going on the other side of the field, wholly out of the factory district. We were not much displeased, however, since there were no people between us and our sinister source of supplies. The walk was a trifle long, but we could haul our silent specimens undisturbed.

Our practice was surprisingly large from the very first—large enough to please most young doctors, and large enough to prove a bore and a burden to students whose real interest lay elsewhere. The mill-hands were of somewhat turbulent inclinations; and besides their many natural needs, their frequent clashes and stabbing affrays gave us plenty to do. But what actually absorbed our minds was the secret laboratory we had fitted up in the cellar—the laboratory with the long table under the electric lights, where in the small hours of the morning we often injected West's various solutions into the veins of the things we dragged from the potter's field. West was experimenting madly to find something which would start man's vital motions anew after they had been stopped by the thing we call death, but had encountered the most ghastly obstacles. The solution had to be differently compounded for different types—what would serve for guinea-pigs would not serve for human beings, and different human specimens required large modifications.

The bodies had to be exceedingly fresh, or the slight decomposition of brain tissue would render perfect reanimation impossible. Indeed, the greatest problem was to get them fresh enough—West had had horrible experiences during his secret college researches with corpses of doubtful vintage. The results of partial or imperfect animation were much more hideous than were the total failures, and we both held fearsome recollections of such things. Ever since our first daemoniac session in the deserted farmhouse on Meadow Hill in Arkham, we had felt a brooding menace; and West, though a calm, blond, blue-eyed scientific automaton in most respects, often confessed to a shuddering sensation of stealthy pursuit. He half felt that he was followed—a psychological delusion of shaken nerves, enhanced by the undeniably disturbing fact that at least one of our reanimated specimens was still alive—a frightful carnivorous thing in a padded cell at Sefton. Then there was another—our first—whose exact fate we had never learned.

We had fair luck with specimens in Bolton—much better than in Arkham. We had not been settled a week before we got an accident victim on the very night of burial, and made it open its eyes with an amazingly rational expression before the solution failed. It had lost an arm—if it had been a perfect body we might have succeeded better. Between then and the next January we secured three more; one total failure, one case of marked muscular motion, and one rather shivery thing—it rose of itself and uttered a sound. Then came a period when luck was poor; interments fell off, and those that did occur were of specimens either too diseased or too maimed for use. We kept track of all the deaths and their circumstances with systematic care.

One March night, however, we unexpectedly obtained a specimen which did not come from the potter's field. In Bolton the prevailing spirit of Puritanism had outlawed the sport of boxing—with the usual result. Surreptitious and ill-conducted bouts among the mill-workers were common, and occasionally professional talent of low grade was imported. This late winter night there had been such a match; evidently with disastrous results, since two timorous Poles had come to us with incoherently whispered entreaties to attend to a very secret and desperate case. We followed them to an abandoned barn, where the remnants of a crowd of frightened foreigners were watching a silent black form on the floor.

The match had been between Kid O'Brien—a lubberly and now quaking youth with a most un-Hibernian hooked nose—and Buck Robinson, "The Harlem Smoke." The negro had been knocked out, and a moment's examination shewed us that he would permanently remain so. He was a loathsome, gorilla-like thing, with abnormally long arms which I could not help calling fore legs, and a face that conjured up thoughts of unspeakable Congo secrets and tom-tom poundings under an eerie moon. The body must have looked even worse in life—but the world holds many ugly things. Fear was upon the whole pitiful crowd, for they did not know what the law would exact of them if the affair were not hushed up; and they were grateful when West, in spite of my involuntary shudders, offered to get rid of the thing quietly—for a purpose I knew too well.

There was bright moonlight over the snowless landscape, but we dressed the thing and carried it home between us through the deserted streets and meadows, as we had carried a similar thing one horrible night in Arkham. We approached the house from the field in the rear, took the specimen in the back door and down the cellar stairs, and prepared it for the usual experiment. Our fear of the police was absurdly great, though we had timed our trip to avoid the solitary patrolman of that section.

The result was wearily anticlimactic. Ghastly as our prize appeared, it was wholly unresponsive to every solution we injected in its black arm; solutions prepared from experience with white specimens only. So as the hour grew dangerously near to dawn, we did as we had done with the others—dragged the thing across the meadows to the neck of the woods near the potter's field, and buried it there in the best sort of grave the frozen ground would furnish. The grave was not very deep, but fully as good as that of the previous specimen—the thing which had risen of itself and uttered a sound. In the light of our dark lanterns we carefully covered it with leaves and dead vines, fairly certain that the police would never find it in a forest so dim and dense.

The next day I was increasingly apprehensive about the police, for a patient brought rumours of a suspected fight and death. West had still another source of worry, for he had been called in the afternoon to a case which ended very threateningly. An Italian woman had become hysterical over her missing child—a lad of five who had strayed off early in the morning and failed to appear for dinner—and had developed symptoms highly alarming in view of an always weak heart. It was a very foolish hysteria, for the boy had often run away before; but Italian peasants are exceedingly superstitious, and this woman seemed as much harassed by omens as by facts. About seven o'clock in the evening she had died, and her frantic husband had made a frightful scene in his efforts to kill West, whom he wildly blamed for not saving her life. Friends had held him when he drew a stiletto, but West departed amidst his inhuman shrieks, curses, and oaths of vengeance. In his latest affliction the fellow seemed to have forgotten his child, who was still missing as the night advanced. There was some talk of searching the woods, but most of the family's friends were busy with the dead woman and the screaming man. Altogether, the nervous strain upon West must have been tremendous. Thoughts of the police and of the mad Italian both weighed heavily.

We retired about eleven, but I did not sleep well. Bolton had a surprisingly good police force for so small a town, and I could not help fearing the mess which would ensue if the affair of the night before were ever tracked down. It might mean the end of all our local work—and perhaps prison for both West and me. I did not like those rumours of a fight which were floating about. After the clock had struck three the moon shone in my eyes, but I turned over without rising to pull down the shade. Then came the steady rattling at the back door.

I lay still and somewhat dazed, but before long heard West's rap on my door. He was clad in dressing-gown and slippers, and had in his hands a revolver and an electric flashlight. From the revolver I knew that he was thinking more of the crazed Italian than of the police.

"We'd better both go," he whispered. "It wouldn't do not to answer it anyway, and it may be a patient—it would be like one of those fools to try the back door."

So we both went down the stairs on tiptoe, with a fear partly justified and partly that which comes only from the soul of the weird small hours. The rattling continued, growing somewhat louder. When we reached the door I cautiously unbolted it and threw it open, and as the moon streamed revealingly down on the form silhouetted there, West did a peculiar thing. Despite the obvious danger of attracting notice and bringing down on our heads the dreaded police investigation—a thing which after all was mercifully averted by the relative isolation of our cottage—my friend suddenly, excitedly, and unnecessarily emptied all six chambers of his revolver into the nocturnal visitor.

For that visitor was neither Italian nor policeman. Looming hideously against the spectral moon was a gigantic misshapen thing not to be imagined save in nightmares—a glassy-eyed, ink-black apparition nearly on all fours, covered with bits of mould, leaves, and vines, foul with caked blood, and having between its glistening teeth a snow-white, terrible, cylindrical object terminating in a tiny hand.

IV. The Scream of the Dead

The scream of a dead man gave to me that acute and added horror of Dr. Herbert West which harassed the latter years of our companionship. It is natural that such a thing as a dead man's scream should give horror, for it is obviously not a pleasing or ordinary occurrence; but I was used to similar experiences, hence suffered on this occasion only because of a particular circumstance. And, as I have implied, it was not of the dead man himself that I became afraid.

Herbert West, whose associate and assistant I was, possessed scientific interests far beyond the usual routine of a village physician. That was why, when establishing his practice in Bolton, he had chosen an isolated house near the potter's field. Briefly and brutally stated, West's sole absorbing interest was a secret study of the phenomena of life and its cessation, leading toward the reanimation of the dead through injections of an excitant solution. For this ghastly experimenting it was necessary to have a constant supply of very fresh human bodies; very fresh because even the least decay hopelessly damaged the brain structure, and human because we found that the solution had to be compounded differently for different types of organisms. Scores of rabbits and guinea-pigs had been killed and treated, but their trail was a blind one. West had never fully succeeded because he had never been able to secure a corpse sufficiently fresh. What he wanted were bodies from which vitality had only just departed; bodies with every cell intact and capable of receiving again the impulse toward that mode of motion called life. There was hope that this second and artificial life might be made perpetual by repetitions of the injection, but we had learned that an ordinary natural life would not respond to the action. To establish the artificial motion, natural life must be extinct—the specimens must be very fresh, but genuinely dead.

The awesome quest had begun when West and I were students at the Miskatonic University Medical School in Arkham, vividly conscious for the first time of the thoroughly mechanical nature of life. That was seven years before, but West looked scarcely a day older now—he was small, blond, clean-shaven, soft-voiced, and spectacled, with only an occasional flash of a cold blue eye to tell of the hardening and growing fanaticism of his character under the pressure of his terrible investigations. Our experiences had often been hideous in the extreme; the results of defective reanimation, when lumps of graveyard clay had been galvanised into morbid, unnatural, and brainless motion by various modifications of the vital solution.

One thing had uttered a nerve-shattering scream; another had risen violently, beaten us both to unconsciousness, and run amuck in a shocking way before it could be placed behind asylum bars; still another, a loathsome African monstrosity, had clawed out of its shallow grave and done a deed—West had had to shoot that object. We could not get bodies fresh enough to shew any trace of reason when reanimated, so had perforce created nameless horrors. It was disturbing to think that one, perhaps two, of our monsters still lived—that thought haunted us shadowingly, till finally West disappeared under frightful circumstances. But at the time of the scream in the cellar laboratory of the isolated Bolton cottage, our fears were subordinate to our anxiety for extremely fresh specimens. West was more avid than I, so that it almost seemed to me that he looked half-covetously at any very healthy living physique.

It was in July, 1910, that the bad luck regarding specimens began to turn. I had been on a long visit to my parents in Illinois, and upon my return found West in a state of singular elation. He had, he told me excitedly, in all likelihood solved the problem of freshness through an approach from an entirely new angle—that of artificial preservation. I had known that he was working on a new and highly unusual embalming compound, and was not surprised that it had turned out well; but until he explained the details I was rather puzzled as to how such a compound could help in our work, since the objectionable staleness of the specimens was largely due to delay occurring before we secured them. This, I now saw, West had clearly recognised; creating his embalming compound for future rather than immediate use, and trusting to fate to supply again some very recent and unburied corpse, as it had years before when we obtained the negro killed in the Bolton prize-fight. At last fate had been kind, so that on this occasion there lay in the secret cellar laboratory a corpse whose decay could not by any possibility have begun. What would happen on reanimation, and whether we could hope for a revival of mind and reason, West did not venture to predict. The experiment would be a landmark in our studies, and he had saved the new body for my return, so that both might share the spectacle in accustomed fashion.

West told me how he had obtained the specimen. It had been a vigorous man; a well-dressed stranger just off the train on his way to transact some business with the Bolton Worsted Mills. The walk through the town had been long, and by the time the traveller paused at our cottage to ask the way to the factories his heart had become greatly overtaxed. He had refused a stimulant, and had suddenly dropped dead only a moment later. The body, as might be expected, seemed to West a heaven-sent gift. In his brief conversation the stranger had made it clear that he was unknown in Bolton, and a search of his pockets subsequently revealed him to be one Robert Leavitt of St. Louis, apparently without a family to make instant inquiries about his disappearance. If this man could not be restored to life, no one would know of our experiment. We buried our materials in a dense strip of woods between the house and the potter's field. If, on the other hand, he could be restored, our fame would be brilliantly and perpetually established. So without delay West had injected into the body's wrist the compound which would hold it fresh for use after my arrival. The matter of the presumably weak heart, which to my mind imperiled the success of our experiment, did not appear to trouble West extensively. He hoped at last to obtain what he had never obtained before—a rekindled spark of reason and perhaps a normal, living creature.

So on the night of July 18, 1910, Herbert West and I stood in the cellar laboratory and gazed at a white, silent figure beneath the dazzling arc-light. The embalming compound had worked uncannily well, for as I stared fascinatedly at the sturdy frame which had lain two weeks without stiffening I was moved to seek West's assurance that the thing was really dead. This assurance he gave readily enough; reminding me that the reanimating solution was never used without careful tests as to life; since it could have no effect if any of the original vitality were present. As West proceeded to take preliminary steps, I was impressed by the vast intricacy of the new experiment; an intricacy so vast that he could trust no hand less delicate than his own. Forbidding me to touch the body, he first injected a drug in the wrist just beside the place his needle had punctured when injecting the embalming compound. This, he said, was to neutralise the compound and release the system to a normal relaxation so that the reanimating solution might freely work when injected. Slightly later, when a change and a gentle tremor seemed to affect the dead limbs, West stuffed a pillow-like object violently over the twitching face, not withdrawing it until the corpse appeared quiet and ready for our attempt at reanimation. The pale enthusiast now applied some last perfunctory tests for absolute lifelessness, withdrew satisfied, and finally injected into the left arm an accurately measured amount of the vital elixir, prepared during the afternoon with a greater care than we had used since college days, when our feats were new and groping. I cannot express the wild, breathless suspense with which we waited for results on this first really fresh specimen—the first we could reasonably expect to open its lips in rational speech, perhaps to tell of what it had seen beyond the unfathomable abyss.

West was a materialist, believing in no soul and attributing all the working of consciousness to bodily phenomena; consequently he looked for no revelation of hideous secrets from gulfs and caverns beyond death's barrier. I did not wholly disagree with him theoretically, yet held vague instinctive remnants of the primitive faith of my forefathers; so that I could not help eyeing the corpse with a certain amount of awe and terrible expectation. Besides—I could not extract from my memory that hideous, inhuman shriek we heard on the night we tried our first experiment in the deserted farmhouse at Arkham.

Very little time had elapsed before I saw the attempt was not to be a total failure. A touch of colour came to cheeks hitherto chalk-white, and spread out under the curiously ample stubble of sandy beard. West, who had his hand on the pulse of the left wrist, suddenly nodded significantly; and almost simultaneously a mist appeared on the mirror inclined above the body's mouth. There followed a few spasmodic muscular motions, and then an audible breathing and visible motion of the chest. I looked at the closed eyelids, and thought I detected a quivering. Then the lids opened, shewing eyes which were grey, calm, and alive, but still unintelligent and not even curious.

In a moment of fantastic whim I whispered questions to the reddening ears; questions of other worlds of which the memory might still be present. Subsequent terror drove them from my mind, but I think the last one, which I repeated, was: "Where have you been?" I do not yet know whether I was answered or not, for no sound came from the well-shaped mouth; but I do know that at that moment I firmly thought the thin lips moved silently, forming syllables I would have vocalised as "only now" if that phrase had possessed any sense or relevancy. At that moment, as I say, I was elated with the conviction that the one great goal had been attained; and that for the first time a reanimated corpse had uttered distinct words impelled by actual reason. In the next moment there was no doubt about the triumph; no doubt that the solution had truly accomplished, at least temporarily, its full mission of restoring rational and articulate life to the dead. But in that triumph there came to me the greatest of all horrors—not horror of the thing that spoke, but of the deed that I had witnessed and of the man with whom my professional fortunes were joined.

For that very fresh body, at last writhing into full and terrifying consciousness with eyes dilated at the memory of its last scene on earth, threw out its frantic hands in a life and death struggle with the air; and suddenly collapsing into a second and final dissolution from which there could be no return, screamed out the cry that will ring eternally in my aching brain:

"Help! Keep off, you cursed little tow-head fiend—keep that damned needle away from me!"

V. The Horror from the Shadows

Many men have related hideous things, not mentioned in print, which happened on the battlefields of the Great War. Some of these things have made me faint, others have convulsed me with devastating nausea, while still others have made me tremble and look behind me in the dark; yet despite the worst of them I believe I can myself relate the most hideous thing of all—the shocking, the unnatural, the unbelievable horror from the shadows.

In 1915 I was a physician with the rank of First Lieutenant in a Canadian regiment in Flanders, one of many Americans to precede the government itself into the gigantic struggle. I had not entered the army on my own initiative, but rather as a natural result of the enlistment of the man whose indispensable assistant I was—the celebrated Boston surgical specialist, Dr. Herbert West. Dr. West had been avid for a chance to serve as surgeon in a great war, and when the chance had come he carried me with him almost against my will. There were reasons why I would have been glad to let the war separate us; reasons why I found the practice of medicine and the companionship of West more and more irritating; but when he had gone to Ottawa and through a colleague's influence secured a medical commission as Major, I could not resist the imperious persuasion of one determined that I should accompany him in my usual capacity.

When I say that Dr. West was avid to serve in battle, I do not mean to imply that he was either naturally warlike or anxious for the safety of civilisation. Always an ice-cold intellectual machine; slight, blond, blue-eyed, and spectacled; I think he secretly sneered at my occasional martial enthusiasms and censures of supine neutrality. There was, however, something he wanted in embattled Flanders; and in order to secure it he had to assume a military exterior. What he wanted was not a thing which many persons want, but something connected with the peculiar branch of medical science which he had chosen quite clandestinely to follow, and in which he had achieved amazing and occasionally hideous results. It was, in fact, nothing more or less than an abundant supply of freshly killed men in every stage of dismemberment.

Herbert West needed fresh bodies because his life-work was the reanimation of the dead. This work was not known to the fashionable clientele who had so swiftly built up his fame after his arrival in Boston; but was only too well known to me, who had been his closest friend and sole assistant since the old days in Miskatonic University

Medical School at Arkham. It was in those college days that he had begun his terrible experiments, first on small animals and then on human bodies shockingly obtained. There was a solution which he injected into the veins of dead things, and if they were fresh enough they responded in strange ways. He had had much trouble in discovering the proper formula, for each type of organism was found to need a stimulus especially adapted to it. Terror stalked him when he reflected on his partial failures; nameless things resulting from imperfect solutions or from bodies insufficiently fresh. A certain number of these failures had remained alive—one was in an asylum while others had vanished—and as he thought of conceivable yet virtually impossible eventualities he often shivered beneath his usual stolidity.

West had soon learned that absolute freshness was the prime requisite for useful specimens, and had accordingly resorted to frightful and unnatural expedients in body-snatching. In college, and during our early practice together in the factory town of Bolton, my attitude toward him had been largely one of fascinated admiration; but as his boldness in methods grew, I began to develop a gnawing fear. I did not like the way he looked at healthy living bodies; and then there came a nightmarish session in the cellar laboratory when I learned that a certain specimen had been a living body when he secured it. That was the first time he had ever been able to revive the quality of rational thought in a corpse; and his success, obtained at such a loathsome cost, had completely hardened him.

Of his methods in the intervening five years I dare not speak. I was held to him by sheer force of fear, and witnessed sights that no human tongue could repeat. Gradually I came to find Herbert West himself more horrible than anything he did—that was when it dawned on me that his once normal scientific zeal for prolonging life had subtly degenerated into a mere morbid and ghoulish curiosity and secret sense of charnel picturesqueness. His interest became a hellish and perverse addiction to the repellently and fiendishly abnormal; he gloated calmly over artificial monstrosities which would make most healthy men drop dead from fright and disgust; he became, behind his pallid intellectuality, a fastidious Baudelaire of physical experiment— a languid Elagabalus of the tombs.

Dangers he met unflinchingly; crimes he committed unmoved. I think the climax came when he had proved his point that rational life can be restored, and had sought new worlds to conquer by experimenting on the reanimation of detached parts of bodies. He had wild and original ideas on the independent vital properties of organic cells and nerve-tissue separated from natural physiological systems; and achieved some hideous preliminary results in the form of never-dying, artificially nourished tissue obtained from the nearly hatched eggs of an indescribable tropical reptile. Two biological points he was exceedingly anxious to settle—first, whether any amount of consciousness and rational action be possible without the brain, proceeding from the spinal cord and various nerve-centres; and second, whether any kind of ethereal, intangible relation distinct from the material cells may exist to link the surgically separated parts of what has previously been a single living organism. All this research work required a prodigious supply of freshly slaughtered human flesh—and that was why Herbert West had entered the Great War.

The phantasmal, unmentionable thing occurred one midnight late in March, 1915, in a field hospital behind the lines at St. Eloi. I wonder even now if it could have been other than a daemoniac dream of delirium. West had a private laboratory in an east room of the barn-like temporary edifice, assigned him on his plea that he was devising new and radical methods for the treatment of hitherto hopeless cases of maiming. There he worked like a butcher in the midst of his gory wares—I could never get used to the levity with which he handled and classified certain things. At times he actually did perform marvels of surgery for the soldiers; but his chief delights were of a less public and philanthropic kind, requiring many explanations of sounds which seemed peculiar even amidst that babel of the damned. Among these sounds were frequent revolver-shots—surely not uncommon on a battlefield, but distinctly uncommon in an hospital. Dr. West's reanimated specimens were not meant for long existence or a large audience. Besides human tissue, West employed much of the reptile embryo tissue which he had cultivated with such singular results. It was better than human material for maintaining life in organless fragments, and that was now my friend's chief activity. In a dark corner of the laboratory, over a queer incubating burner, he kept a large covered vat full of this reptilian cell-matter; which multiplied and grew puffily and hideously.

On the night of which I speak we had a splendid new specimen—a man at once physically powerful and of such high mentality that a sensitive nervous system was assured. It was rather ironic, for he was the officer who had helped West to his commission, and who was now to have been our associate. Moreover, he had in the past secretly studied the theory of reanimation to some extent under West. Major

Sir Eric Moreland Clapham-Lee, D.S.O., was the greatest surgeon in our division, and had been hastily assigned to the St. Eloi sector when news of the heavy fighting reached headquarters. He had come in an aeroplane piloted by the intrepid Lieut. Ronald Hill, only to be shot down when directly over his destination. The fall had been spectacular and awful; Hill was unrecognisable afterward, but the wreck yielded up the great surgeon in a nearly decapitated but otherwise intact condition. West had greedily seized the lifeless thing which had once been his friend and fellow-scholar; and I shuddered when he finished severing the head, placed it in his hellish vat of pulpy reptile-tissue to preserve it for future experiments, and proceeded to treat the decapitated body on the operating table. He injected new blood, joined certain veins, arteries, and nerves at the headless neck, and closed the ghastly aperture with engrafted skin from an unidentified specimen which had borne an officer's uniform. I knew what he wanted—to see if this highly organised body could exhibit, without its head, any of the signs of mental life which had distinguished Sir Eric Moreland Clapham-Lee. Once a student of reanimation, this silent trunk was now gruesomely called upon to exemplify it.

I can still see Herbert West under the sinister electric light as he injected his reanimating solution into the arm of the headless body. The scene I cannot describe—I should faint if I tried it, for there is madness in a room full of classified charnel things, with blood and lesser human debris almost ankle-deep on the slimy floor, and with hideous reptilian abnormalities sprouting, bubbling, and baking over a winking bluish-green spectre of dim flame in a far corner of black shadows.

The specimen, as West repeatedly observed, had a splendid nervous system. Much was expected of it; and as a few twitching motions began to appear, I could see the feverish interest on West's face. He was ready, I think, to see proof of his increasingly strong opinion that consciousness, reason, and personality can exist independently of the brain—that man has no central connective spirit, but is merely a machine of nervous matter, each section more or less complete in itself. In one triumphant demonstration West was about to relegate the mystery of life to the category of myth. The body now twitched more vigorously, and beneath our avid eyes commenced to heave in a frightful way. The arms stirred disquietingly, the legs drew up, and various muscles contracted in a repulsive kind of writhing. Then the headless thing threw out its arms in a gesture which was unmistakably one of desperation—an intelligent desperation apparently sufficient to prove every theory of Herbert West. Certainly, the nerves were recalling the man's last act in life; the struggle to get free of the falling aeroplane.

What followed, I shall never positively know. It may have been wholly an hallucination from the shock caused at that instant by the sudden and complete destruction of the building in a cataclysm of German shell-fire—who can gainsay it, since West and I were the only proved survivors? West liked to think that before his recent disappearance, but there were times when he could not; for it was queer that we both had the same hallucination. The hideous occurrence itself was very simple, notable only for what it implied.

The body on the table had risen with a blind and terrible groping, and we had heard a sound. I should not call that sound a voice, for it was too awful. And yet its timbre was not the most awful thing about it. Neither was its message—it had merely screamed, "Jump, Ronald, for God's sake, jump!" The awful thing was its source.

For it had come from the large covered vat in that ghoulish corner of crawling black shadows.

VI. The Tomb-Legions

When Dr. Herbert West disappeared a year ago, the Boston police questioned me closely. They suspected that I was holding something back, and perhaps suspected graver things; but I could not tell them the truth because they would not have believed it. They knew, indeed, that West had been connected with activities beyond the credence of ordinary men; for his hideous experiments in the reanimation of dead bodies had long been too extensive to admit of perfect secrecy; but the final soul-shattering catastrophe held elements of daemoniac phantasy which make even me doubt the reality of what I saw.

I was West's closest friend and only confidential assistant. We had met years before, in medical school, and from the first I had shared his terrible researches. He had slowly tried to perfect a solution which, injected into the veins of the newly deceased, would restore life; a labour demanding an abundance of fresh corpses and therefore involving the most unnatural actions. Still more shocking were the products of some of the experiments—grisly masses of flesh that had been dead, but that West waked to a blind, brainless, nauseous animation. These were the usual results, for in order to reawaken the mind it was necessary to have specimens so absolutely fresh that no decay could possibly affect the delicate brain-cells.

This need for very fresh corpses had been West's moral undoing. They were hard to get, and one awful day he had secured his specimen while it was still alive and vigorous. A struggle, a needle, and a powerful alkaloid had transformed it to a very fresh corpse, and the experiment had succeeded for a brief and memorable moment; but West had emerged with a soul calloused and seared, and a hardened eye which sometimes glanced with a kind of hideous and calculating appraisal at men of especially sensitive brain and especially vigorous physique. Toward the last I became acutely afraid of West, for he began to look at me that way. People did not seem to notice his glances, but they noticed my fear; and after his disappearance used that as a basis for some absurd suspicions.

West, in reality, was more afraid than I; for his abominable pursuits entailed a life of furtiveness and dread of every shadow. Partly it was the police he feared; but sometimes his nervousness was deeper and more nebulous, touching on certain indescribable things into which he had injected a morbid life, and from which he had not seen that life depart. He usually finished his experiments with a revolver, but a few times he had not been quick enough. There was that first specimen on whose rifled grave marks of clawing were later seen. There was also that Arkham professor's body which had done cannibal things before it had been captured and thrust unidentified into a madhouse cell at Sefton, where it beat the walls for sixteen years. Most of the other possibly surviving results were things less easy to speak of—for in later years West's scientific zeal had degenerated to an unhealthy and fantastic mania, and he had spent his chief skill in vitalising not entire human bodies but isolated parts of bodies, or parts joined to organic matter other than human. It had become fiendishly disgusting by the time he disappeared; many of the experiments could not even be hinted at in print. The Great War, through which both of us served as surgeons, had intensified this side of West.

In saying that West's fear of his specimens was nebulous, I have in mind particularly its complex nature. Part of it came merely from knowing of the existence of such nameless monsters, while another part arose from apprehension of the bodily harm they might under certain circumstances do him. Their disappearance added horror to the situation—of them all West knew the whereabouts of only one, the pitiful asylum thing. Then there was a more subtle fear—a very fantastic sensation resulting from a curious experiment in the Canadian army in 1915. West, in the midst of a severe battle, had reanimated Major Sir Eric Moreland Clapham-Lee, D.S.O., a fellow-physician who knew about his experiments and could have duplicated them. The head had been removed, so that the possibilities of quasi-intelligent life in the trunk might be investigated. Just as the building was wiped out by a German shell, there had been a success. The trunk had moved intelligently; and, unbelievable to relate, we were both sickeningly sure that articulate sounds had come from the detached head as it lay in a shadowy corner of the laboratory. The shell had been merciful, in a way—but West could never feel as certain as he wished, that we two were the only survivors. He used to make shuddering conjectures about the possible actions of a headless physician with the power of reanimating the dead.

West's last quarters were in a venerable house of much elegance, overlooking one of the oldest burying-grounds in Boston. He had chosen the place for purely symbolic and fantastically aesthetic reasons, since most of the interments were of the colonial period and therefore of little use to a scientist seeking very fresh bodies. The laboratory was in a sub-cellar secretly constructed by imported workmen, and contained a huge incinerator for the quiet and complete disposal of such bodies, or fragments and synthetic mockeries of bodies, as might remain from the morbid experiments and unhallowed amusements of the owner. During the excavation of this cellar the workmen had struck some exceedingly ancient masonry; undoubtedly connected with the old burying-ground, yet far too deep to correspond with any known sepulchre therein. After a number of calculations West decided that it represented some secret chamber beneath the tomb of the Averills, where the last interment had been made in 1768. I was with him when he studied the nitrous, dripping walls laid bare by the spades and mattocks of the men, and was prepared for the gruesome thrill which would attend the uncovering of centuried grave-secrets; but for the first time West's new timidity conquered his natural curiosity, and he betrayed his degenerating fibre by ordering the masonry left intact and plastered over. Thus it remained till that final hellish night; part of the walls of the secret laboratory. I speak of West's decadence, but must add that it was a purely mental and intangible thing. Outwardly he was the same to the last—calm, cold, slight, and yellow-haired, with spectacled blue eyes and a general aspect of youth which years and fears seemed never to change. He seemed calm even when he thought of that clawed grave and looked over his shoulder; even when he thought of the carnivorous thing that gnawed and pawed at Sefton bars.

The end of Herbert West began one evening in our joint study when he was dividing his curious glance between the newspaper and me. A strange headline item had struck at him from the crumpled pages, and a nameless titan claw had seemed to reach down through sixteen years. Something fearsome and incredible had happened at Sefton Asylum fifty miles away, stunning the neighbourhood and baffling the police. In the small hours of the morning a body of silent men had entered the grounds and their leader had aroused the attendants. He was a menacing military figure who talked without moving his lips and whose voice seemed almost ventriloquially connected with an immense black case he carried. His expressionless face was handsome to the point of radiant beauty, but had shocked the superintendent when the hall light fell on it—for it was a wax face with eyes of painted glass. Some nameless accident had befallen this man. A larger man guided his steps; a repellent hulk whose bluish face seemed half eaten away by some unknown malady. The speaker had asked for the custody of the cannibal monster committed from Arkham sixteen years before; and upon being refused, gave a signal which precipitated a shocking riot. The fiends had beaten, trampled, and bitten every attendant who did not flee; killing four and finally succeeding in the liberation of the monster. Those victims who could recall the event without hysteria swore that the creatures had acted less like men than like unthinkable automata guided by the wax-faced leader. By the time help could be summoned, every trace of the men and of their mad charge had vanished.

From the hour of reading this item until midnight, West sat almost paralysed. At midnight the doorbell rang, startling him fearfully. All the servants were asleep in the attic, so I answered the bell. As I have told the police, there was no wagon in the street; but only a group of strange-looking figures bearing a large square box which they deposited in the hallway after one of them had grunted in a highly unnatural voice, "Express—prepaid." They filed out of the house with a jerky tread, and as I watched them go I had an odd idea that they were turning toward the ancient cemetery on which the back of the house abutted. When I slammed the door after them West came downstairs and looked at the box. It was about two feet square, and bore West's correct name and present address. It also bore the inscription, "From Eric Moreland Clapham-Lee, St. Eloi, Flanders." Six years before, in Flanders, a shelled hospital had fallen upon the headless reanimated trunk of Dr. Clapham-Lee, and upon the detached head which—perhaps—had uttered articulate sounds.

West was not even excited now. His condition was more ghastly. Quickly he said, "It's the finish—but let's incinerate—this." We carried the thing down to the laboratory—listening. I do not remember many particulars—you can imagine my state of mind—but it is a vicious lie to say it was Herbert West's body which I put into the incinerator. We both inserted the whole unopened wooden box, closed the door, and started the electricity. Nor did any sound come from the box, after all.

It was West who first noticed the falling plaster on that part of the wall where the ancient tomb masonry had been covered up. I was going to run, but he stopped me. Then I saw a small black aperture, felt a ghoulish wind of ice, and smelled the charnel bowels of a putrescent earth. There was no sound, but just then the electric lights went out and I saw outlined against some phosphorescence of the nether world a horde of silent toiling things which only insanity—or worse—could create. Their outlines were human, semi-human, fractionally human, and not human at all—the horde was grotesquely heterogeneous. They were removing the stones quietly, one by one, from the centuried wall. And then, as the breach became large enough, they came out into the laboratory in single file; led by a stalking thing with a beautiful head made of wax. A sort of mad-eyed monstrosity behind the leader seized on Herbert West. West did not resist or utter a sound. Then they all sprang at him and tore him to pieces before my eyes, bearing the fragments away into that subterranean vault of fabulous abominations. West's head was carried off by the wax-headed leader, who wore a Canadian officer's uniform. As it disappeared I saw that the blue eyes behind the spectacles were hideously blazing with their first touch of frantic, visible emotion.

Servants found me unconscious in the morning. West was gone. The incinerator contained only unidentifiable ashes. Detectives have questioned me, but what can I say? The Sefton tragedy they will not connect with West; not that, nor the men with the box, whose existence they deny. I told them of the vault, and they pointed to the unbroken plaster wall and laughed. So I told them no more. They imply that I am a madman or a murderer—probably I am mad. But I might not be mad if those accursed tomb-legions had not been so silent.

Pickman's Model

You needn't think I'm crazy, Eliot—plenty of others have queerer prejudices than this. Why don't you laugh at Oliver's grandfather, who won't ride in a motor? If I don't like that damned subway, it's my own business; and we got here more quickly anyhow in the taxi. We'd have had to walk up the hill from Park Street if we'd taken the car.

I know I'm more nervous than I was when you saw me last year, but you don't need to hold a clinic over it. There's plenty of reason, God knows, and I fancy I'm lucky to be sane at all. Why the third degree? You didn't use to be so inquisitive.

Well, if you must hear it, I don't know why you shouldn't. Maybe you ought to, anyhow, for you kept writing me like a grieved parent when you heard I'd begun to cut the Art Club and keep away from Pickman. Now that he's disappeared I go around to the club once in a while, but my nerves aren't what they were.

No, I don't know what's become of Pickman, and I don't like to guess. You might have surmised I had some inside information when I dropped him—and that's why I don't want to think where he's gone. Let the police find what they can—it won't be much, judging from the fact that they don't know yet of the old North End place he hired under the name of Peters. I'm not sure that I could find it again myself—not that I'd ever try, even in broad daylight! Yes, I do know, or am afraid I know, why he maintained it. I'm coming to that. And I think you'll understand before I'm through why I don't tell the police. They would ask me to guide them, but I couldn't go back there even if I knew the way. There was something there—and now I can't use the subway or (and you may as well have your laugh at this, too) go down into cellars any more.

I should think you'd have known I didn't drop Pickman for the same silly reasons that fussy old women like Dr. Reid or Joe Minot or Bosworth did. Morbid art doesn't shock me, and when a man has the genius Pickman had I feel it an honour to know him, no matter what direction his work takes. Boston never had a greater painter than Richard Upton Pickman. I said it at first and I say it still, and I never swerved an inch, either, when he shewed that "Ghoul Feeding." That, you remember, was when Minot cut him.

You know, it takes profound art and profound insight into Nature to turn out stuff like Pickman's. Any magazine-cover hack can splash paint around wildly and call it a nightmare or a Witches' Sabbath or a portrait of the devil, but only a great painter can make such a thing really scare or ring true. That's because only a real artist knows the actual anatomy of the terrible or the physiology of fear—the exact sort of lines and proportions that connect up with latent instincts or hereditary memories of fright, and the proper colour contrasts and lighting effects to stir the dormant sense of strangeness. I don't have to tell you why a Fuseli really brings a shiver while a cheap ghost-story frontispiece merely makes us laugh. There's something those fellows catch—beyond life—that they're able to make us catch for a second. Doré had it. Sime has it. Angarola of Chicago has it. And Pickman had it as no man ever had it before or—I hope to heaven—ever will again.

Don't ask me what it is they see. You know, in ordinary art, there's all the difference in the world between the vital, breathing things drawn from Nature or models and the artificial truck that commercial small fry reel off in a bare studio by rule. Well, I should say that the really weird artist has a kind of vision which makes models, or summons up what amounts to actual scenes from the spectral world he lives in. Anyhow, he manages to turn out results that differ from the pretender's mince-pie dreams in just about the same way that the life painter's results differ from the concoctions of a correspondence-school cartoonist. If I had ever seen what Pickman saw—but no! Here, let's have a drink before we get any deeper. Gad, I wouldn't be alive if I'd ever seen what that man—if he was a man—saw!

You recall that Pickman's forte was faces. I don't believe anybody since Goya could put so much of sheer hell into a set of features or a twist of expression. And before Goya you have to go back to the mediaeval chaps who did the gargoyles and chimaeras on Notre Dame and Mont Saint-Michel. They believed all sorts of things—and maybe they saw all sorts of things, too, for the Middle Ages had some curious phases. I remember your asking Pickman yourself once, the year before you went away, wherever in thunder he got such ideas and visions. Wasn't that a nasty laugh he gave you? It was partly because of that laugh that Reid dropped him. Reid, you know, had just taken up comparative pathology, and was full of pompous "inside stuff" about the biological or evolutionary significance of this or that mental or physical symptom. He said Pickman repelled him more and more every day, and almost frightened him toward the last—that the fellow's features and expression were slowly developing in a way he didn't like; in a way that wasn't human. He had a lot of talk about diet, and said Pickman must be abnormal and eccentric to the last degree. I suppose you told Reid, if you and he had any correspondence over it, that he'd let Pickman's paintings get on his nerves or harrow up his imagination. I know I told him that myself—then.

But keep in mind that I didn't drop Pickman for anything like this. On the contrary, my admiration for him kept growing; for that "Ghoul Feeding" was a tremendous achievement. As you know, the club wouldn't exhibit it, and the Museum of Fine Arts wouldn't accept it as a gift; and I can add that nobody would buy it, so Pickman had it right in his house till he went. Now his father has it in Salem—you know Pickman comes of old Salem stock, and had a witch ancestor hanged in 1692.

I got into the habit of calling on Pickman quite often, especially after I began making notes for a monograph on weird art. Probably it was his work which put the idea into my head, and anyhow, I found him a mine of data and suggestions when I came to develop it. He shewed me all the paintings and drawings he had about; including some pen-and-ink sketches that would, I verily believe, have got him kicked out of the club if many of the members had seen them. Before long I was pretty nearly a devotee, and would listen for hours like a schoolboy to art theories and philosophic speculations wild enough to qualify him for the Danvers asylum. My hero-worship, coupled with the fact that people generally were commencing to have less and less to do with him, made him get very confidential with me; and one evening he hinted that if I were fairly close-mouthed and none too squeamish, he might shew me something rather unusual—something a bit stronger than anything he had in the house.

"You know," he said, "there are things that won't do for Newbury Street—things that are out of place here, and that can't be conceived here, anyhow. It's my business to catch the overtones of the soul, and you won't find those in a parvenu set of artificial streets on made land. Back Bay isn't Boston—it isn't anything yet, because it's had no time to pick up memories and attract local spirits. If there are any ghosts here, they're the tame ghosts of a salt marsh and a shallow cove; and I want human ghosts—the ghosts of beings highly organised enough to have looked on hell and known the meaning of what they saw.

"The place for an artist to live is the North End. If any aesthete were sincere, he'd put up with the slums for the sake of the massed traditions. God, man! Don't you realise that places like that weren't merely *made*, but actually *grew*? Generation after generation lived and felt and died there, and in days when people weren't afraid to live and feel and die. Don't you know there was a mill on Copp's Hill in 1632, and that half the present streets were laid out by 1650? I can shew you houses that have stood two centuries and a half and more; houses that have witnessed what would make a modern house crumble into powder. What do moderns know of life and the forces behind it? You call the Salem witchcraft a delusion, but I'll wage my four-times-great-grandmother could have told you things. They hanged her on Gallows Hill, with Cotton Mather looking sanctimoniously on. Mather, damn him, was afraid somebody might succeed in kicking free of this accursed cage of monotony—I wish someone had laid a spell on him or sucked his blood in the night!

"I can shew you a house he lived in, and I can shew you another one he was afraid to enter in spite of all his fine bold talk. He knew things he didn't dare put into that stupid *Magnalia* or that puerile *Wonders of the Invisible World*. Look here, do you know the whole North End once had a set of tunnels that kept certain people in touch with each other's houses, and the burying-ground, and the sea? Let them prosecute and persecute above ground—things went on every day that they couldn't reach, and voices laughed at night that they couldn't place!

"Why, man, out of ten surviving houses built before 1700 and not moved since I'll wager that in eight I can shew you something queer in the cellar. There's hardly a month that you don't read of workmen finding bricked-up arches and wells leading nowhere in this or that old place as it comes down—you could see one near Henchman Street from the elevated last year. There were witches and what their spells summoned; pirates and what they brought in from the sea; smugglers; privateers—and I tell you, people knew how to live, and how to enlarge the bounds of life, in the old times! This wasn't the only world a bold and wise man could know—faugh! And to think of today in contrast, with such pale-pink brains that even a club of supposed artists gets shudders and convulsions if a picture goes beyond the feelings of a Beacon Street tea-table!

"The only saving grace of the present is that it's too damned stupid to question the past very closely. What do maps and records and guide-books really tell of the North End? Bah! At a guess I'll guarantee to lead you to thirty or forty alleys and networks of alleys north of Prince Street that aren't suspected by ten living beings outside of the foreigners that swarm them. And what do those Dagoes know of their meaning? No, Thurber, these ancient places are dreaming gorgeously and overflowing with wonder and terror and escapes from the commonplace, and yet there's not a living soul to understand or profit by them. Or rather, there's only one living soul—for I haven't been digging around in the past for nothing!

"See here, you're interested in this sort of thing. What if I told you that I've got another studio up there, where I can catch the night-spirit of antique horror and paint things that I couldn't even think of in Newbury Street? Naturally I don't tell those cursed old maids at the club—with Reid, damn him, whispering even as it is that I'm a sort of monster bound down the toboggan of reverse evolution. Yes, Thurber, I decided long ago that one must paint terror as well as beauty from life, so I did some exploring in places where I had reason to know terror lives.

"I've got a place that I don't believe three living Nordic men besides myself have ever seen. It isn't so very far from the elevated as distance goes, but it's centuries away as the soul goes. I took it because of the queer old brick well in the cellar—one of the sort I told you about. The shack's almost tumbling down, so that nobody else would live there, and I'd hate to tell you how little I pay for it. The windows are boarded up, but I like that all the better, since I don't want daylight for what I do. I paint in the cellar, where the inspiration is thickest, but I've other rooms furnished on the ground floor. A Sicilian owns it, and I've hired it under the name of Peters.

"Now if you're game, I'll take you there tonight. I think you'd enjoy the pictures, for as I said, I've let myself go a bit there. It's no vast tour—I sometimes do it on foot, for I don't want to attract attention with a taxi in such a place. We can take the shuttle at the South Station for Battery Street, and after that the walk isn't much."

Well, Eliot, there wasn't much for me to do after that harangue but to keep myself from running instead of walking for the first vacant cab we could sight. We changed to the elevated at the South Station, and at about twelve o'clock had climbed down the steps at Battery Street and struck along the old waterfront past Constitution Wharf. I didn't keep track of the cross streets, and can't tell you yet which it was we turned up, but I know it wasn't Greenough Lane.

When we did turn, it was to climb through the deserted length of the oldest and dirtiest alley I ever saw in my life, with crumbling-looking gables, broken small-paned windows, and archaic chimneys that stood out half-disintegrated against the moonlit sky. I don't believe there were three houses in sight that hadn't been standing in Cotton Mather's time—certainly I glimpsed at least two with an overhang, and once I thought I saw a peaked roof-line of the almost forgotten pre-gambrel type, though antiquarians tell us there are none left in Boston.

From that alley, which had a dim light, we turned to the left into an equally silent and still narrower alley with no light at all; and in a minute made what I think was an obtuse-angled bend toward the right in the dark. Not long after this Pickman produced a flashlight and revealed an antediluvian ten-panelled door that looked damnably worm-eaten. Unlocking it, he ushered me into a barren hallway with what was once splendid dark-oak panelling—simple, of course, but thrillingly suggestive of the times of Andros and Phipps and the Witchcraft. Then he took me through a door on the left, lighted an oil lamp, and told me to make myself at home.

Now, Eliot, I'm what the man in the street would call fairly "hard-boiled", but I'll confess that what I saw on the walls of that room gave me a bad turn. They were his pictures, you know—the ones he couldn't paint or even shew in Newbury Street—and he was right when he said he had "let himself go." Here—have another drink—I need one anyhow!

There's no use in my trying to tell you what they were like, because the awful, the blasphemous horror, and the unbelievable loathsomeness and moral foetor came from simple touches quite beyond the power of words to classify. There was none of the exotic technique you see in Sidney Sime, none of the trans-Saturnian landscapes and lunar fungi that Clark Ashton Smith uses to freeze the blood. The backgrounds were mostly old churchyards, deep woods, cliffs by the sea, brick tunnels, ancient panelled rooms, or simple vaults of masonry. Copp's Hill Burying Ground, which could not be many blocks away from this very house, was a favourite scene.

The madness and monstrosity lay in the figures in the foreground—for Pickman's morbid art was preeminently one of daemoniac portraiture. These figures were seldom completely human, but often approached humanity in varying degree. Most of the bodies, while roughly bipedal, had a forward slumping, and a vaguely canine cast. The texture of the majority was a kind of unpleasant rubberiness. Ugh! I can see them now! Their occupations—well, don't ask me to be too precise. They were usually feeding—I won't say on what. They were sometimes shewn in groups in cemeteries or underground passages, and often appeared to be in battle over their prey—or rather, their treasure-trove. And what damnable expressiveness Pickman sometimes gave the sightless faces of this charnel booty! Occasionally the things were shewn leaping through open windows at night, or squatting on the chests of sleepers, worrying at their throats. One canvas shewed a ring of them baying about a hanged witch on Gallows Hill, whose dead face held a close kinship to theirs.

But don't get the idea that it was all this hideous business of theme and setting which struck me faint. I'm not a three-year-old kid, and I'd seen much like this before. It was the *faces*, Eliot, those accursed *faces*, that leered and slavered out of the canvas with the very breath of life! By God, man, I verily believe they were alive! That nauseous wizard had waked the fires of hell in pigment, and his brush had been a nightmare-spawning wand. Give me that decanter, Eliot!

There was one thing called "The Lesson"—heaven pity me, that I ever saw it! Listen—can you fancy a squatting circle of nameless dog-like things in a churchyard teaching a small child how to feed like themselves? The price of a changeling, I suppose—you know the old myth about how the weird people leave their spawn in cradles in exchange for the human babes they steal. Pickman was shewing what happens to those stolen babes—how they grow up—and then I began to see a hideous relationship in the faces of the human and non-human figures. He was, in all his gradations of morbidity between the frankly non-human and the degradedly human, establishing a sardonic linkage and evolution. The dog-things were developed from mortals!

And no sooner had I wondered what he made of their own young as left with mankind in the form of changelings, than my eye caught a picture embodying that very thought. It was that of an ancient Puritan interior—a heavily beamed room with lattice windows, a settle, and clumsy seventeenth-century furniture, with the family sitting about while the father read from the Scriptures. Every face but one shewed nobility and reverence, but that one reflected the mockery of the pit. It was that of a young man in years, and no doubt belonged to a supposed son of that pious father, but in essence it was the kin of the unclean things. It was their changeling—and in a spirit of supreme irony Pickman had given the features a very perceptible resemblance to his own.

By this time Pickman had lighted a lamp in an adjoining room and was politely holding open the door for me; asking me if I would care to see his "modern studies." I hadn't been able to give him much of my opinions—I was too speechless with fright and loathing—but I think he fully understood and felt highly complimented. And now I want to assure you again, Eliot, that I'm no mollycoddle to scream at anything which shews a bit of departure from the usual. I'm middle-aged and decently sophisticated, and I guess you saw enough of me in France to know I'm not easily knocked out. Remember, too, that I'd just about recovered my wind and gotten used to those frightful pictures which turned colonial New England into a kind of annex of hell. Well, in spite of all this, that next room forced a real scream out of me, and I had to clutch at the doorway to keep from keeling over. The other chamber had shewn a pack of ghouls and witches overrunning the world of our forefathers, but this one brought the horror right into our own daily life!

Gad, how that man could paint! There was a study called "Subway Accident", in which a flock of the vile things were clambering up from some unknown catacomb through a crack in the floor of the Boylston Street subway and attacking a crowd of people on the platform. Another shewed a dance on Copp's Hill among the tombs with the background of today. Then there were any number of cellar views, with monsters creeping in through holes and rifts in the masonry and grinning as they squatted behind barrels or furnaces and waited for their first victim to descend the stairs.

One disgusting canvas seemed to depict a vast cross-section of Beacon Hill, with ant-like armies of the mephitic monsters squeezing themselves through burrows that honeycombed the ground. Dances in the modern cemeteries were freely pictured, and another conception somehow shocked me more than all the rest—a scene in an unknown vault, where scores of the beasts crowded about one who held a well-known Boston guide-book and was evidently reading aloud. All were pointing to a certain passage, and every face seemed so distorted with epileptic and reverberant laughter that I almost thought I heard the fiendish echoes. The title of the picture was, "Holmes, Lowell, and Longfellow Lie Buried in Mount Auburn."

As I gradually steadied myself and got readjusted to this second room of deviltry and morbidity, I began to analyse some of the points in my sickening loathing. In the first place, I said to myself, these things repelled because of the utter inhumanity and callous cruelty they shewed in Pickman. The fellow must be a relentless enemy of all mankind to take such glee in the torture of brain and flesh and the degradation of the mortal tenement. In the second place, they terrified because of their very greatness. Their art was the art that convinced—when we saw the pictures we saw the daemons themselves and were afraid of them. And the queer part was, that Pickman got none of his power from the use of selectiveness or bizarrerie. Nothing was blurred, distorted, or conventionalised;

outlines were sharp and life-like, and details were almost painfully defined. And the faces!

It was not any mere artist's interpretation that we saw; it was pandemonium itself, crystal clear in stark objectivity. That was it, by heaven! The man was not a *fantaisiste* or romanticist at all—he did not even try to give us the churning, prismatic ephemera of dreams, but coldly and sardonically reflected some stable, mechanistic, and well-established horror-world which he saw fully, brilliantly, squarely, and unfalteringly. God knows what that world can have been, or where he ever glimpsed the blasphemous shapes that loped and trotted and crawled through it; but whatever the baffling source of his images, one thing was plain. Pickman was in every sense—in conception and in execution—a thorough, painstaking, and almost scientific realist.

My host was now leading the way down cellar to his actual studio, and I braced myself for some hellish effects among the unfinished canvases. As we reached the bottom of the damp stairs he turned his flashlight to a corner of the large open space at hand, revealing the circular brick curb of what was evidently a great well in the earthen floor. We walked nearer, and I saw that it must be five feet across, with walls a good foot thick and some six inches above the ground level—solid work of the seventeenth century, or I was much mistaken. That, Pickman said, was the kind of thing he had been talking about—an aperture of the network of tunnels that used to undermine the hill. I noticed idly that it did not seem to be bricked up, and that a heavy disc of wood formed the apparent cover. Thinking of the things this well must have been connected with if Pickman's wild hints had not been mere rhetoric, I shivered slightly; then turned to follow him up a step and through a narrow door into a room of fair size, provided with a wooden floor and furnished as a studio. An acetylene gas outfit gave the light necessary for work.

The unfinished pictures on easels or propped against the walls were as ghastly as the finished ones upstairs, and shewed the painstaking methods of the artist. Scenes were blocked out with extreme care, and pencilled guide lines told of the minute exactitude which Pickman used in getting the right perspective and proportions. The man was great—I say it even now, knowing as much as I do. A large camera on a table excited my notice, and Pickman told me that he used it in taking scenes for backgrounds, so that he might paint them from photographs in the studio instead of carting his outfit around the town for this or that view. He thought a photograph quite as good as an actual scene or model for sustained work, and declared he employed them regularly.

There was something very disturbing about the nauseous sketches and half-finished monstrosities that leered around from every side of the room, and when Pickman suddenly unveiled a huge canvas on the side away from the light I could not for my life keep back a loud scream—the second I had emitted that night. It echoed and echoed through the dim vaultings of that ancient and nitrous cellar, and I had to choke back a flood of reaction that threatened to burst out as hysterical laughter. Merciful Creator! Eliot, but I don't know how much was real and how much was feverish fancy. It doesn't seem to me that earth can hold a dream like that!

It was a colossal and nameless blasphemy with glaring red eyes, and it held in bony claws a thing that had been a man, gnawing at the head as a child nibbles at a stick of candy. Its position was a kind of crouch, and as one looked one felt that at any moment it might drop its present prey and seek a juicier morsel. But damn it all, it wasn't even the fiendish subject that made it such an immortal fountain-head of all panic—not that, nor the dog face with its pointed ears, bloodshot eyes, flat nose, and drooling lips. It wasn't the scaly claws nor the mould-caked body nor the half-hooved feet—none of these, though any one of them might well have driven an excitable man to madness.

It was the technique, Eliot—the cursed, the impious, the unnatural technique! As I am a living being, I never elsewhere saw the actual breath of life so fused into a canvas. The monster was there—it glared and gnawed and gnawed and glared—and I knew that only a suspension of Nature's laws could ever let a man paint a thing like that without a model—without some glimpse of the nether world which no mortal unsold to the Fiend has ever had.

Pinned with a thumb-tack to a vacant part of the canvas was a piece of paper now badly curled up—probably, I thought, a photograph from which Pickman meant to paint a background as hideous as the nightmare it was to enhance. I reached out to uncurl and look at it, when suddenly I saw Pickman start as if shot. He had been listening with peculiar intensity ever since my shocked scream had waked unaccustomed echoes in the dark cellar, and now he seemed struck with a fright which, though not comparable to my own, had in it more of the physical than of the spiritual. He drew a revolver and motioned me to silence, then stepped out into the main cellar and closed the door behind him.

I think I was paralysed for an instant. Imitating Pickman's listening, I fancied I heard a faint scurrying sound somewhere, and a series of squeals or bleats in a direction I couldn't determine. I thought of huge rats and shuddered. Then there came a subdued sort of clatter which somehow set me all in gooseflesh—a furtive, groping kind of clatter, though I can't attempt to convey what I mean in words. It was like heavy wood falling on stone or brick—wood on brick—what did that make me think of?

It came again, and louder. There was a vibration as if the wood had fallen farther than it had fallen before. After that followed a sharp grating noise, a shouted gibberish from Pickman, and the deafening discharge of all six chambers of a revolver, fired spectacularly as a lion-tamer might fire in the air for effect. A muffled squeal or squawk, and a thud. Then more wood and brick grating, a pause, and the opening of the door—at which I'll confess I started violently. Pickman reappeared with his smoking weapon, cursing the bloated rats that infested the ancient well.

"The deuce knows what they eat, Thurber," he grinned, "for those archaic tunnels touched graveyard and witch-den and sea-coast. But whatever it is, they must have run short, for they were devilish anxious to get out. Your yelling stirred them up, I fancy. Better be cautious in these old places—our rodent friends are the one drawback, though I sometimes think they're a positive asset by way of atmosphere and colour."

Well, Eliot, that was the end of the night's adventure. Pickman had promised to shew me the place, and heaven knows he had done it. He led me out of that tangle of alleys in another direction, it seems, for when we sighted a lamp post we were in a half-familiar street with monotonous rows of mingled tenement blocks and old houses. Charter Street, it turned out to be, but I was too flustered to notice just where we hit it. We were too late for the elevated, and walked back downtown through Hanover Street. I remember that walk. We switched from Tremont up Beacon, and Pickman left me at the corner of Joy, where I turned off. I never spoke to him again.

Why did I drop him? Don't be impatient. Wait till I ring for coffee. We've had enough of the other stuff, but I for one need something. No—it wasn't the paintings I saw in that place; though I'll swear they were enough to get him ostracised in nine-tenths of the homes and clubs of Boston, and I guess you won't wonder now why I have to steer clear of subways and cellars. It was—something I found in my coat the next morning. You know, the curled-up paper tacked to that frightful canvas in the cellar; the thing I thought was a photograph of some scene he meant to use as a background for that monster. That last scare had come while I was reaching to uncurl it, and it seems I had vacantly crumpled it into my pocket. But here's the coffee—take it black, Eliot, if you're wise.

Yes, that paper was the reason I dropped Pickman; Richard Upton Pickman, the greatest artist I have ever known—and the foulest being that ever leaped the bounds of life into the pits of myth and madness. Eliot—old Reid was right. He wasn't strictly human. Either he was born in strange shadow, or he'd found a way to unlock the forbidden gate. It's all the same now, for he's gone—back into the fabulous darkness he loved to haunt. Here, let's have the chandelier going.

Don't ask me to explain or even conjecture about what I burned. Don't ask me, either, what lay behind that mole-like scrambling Pickman was so keen to pass off as rats. There are secrets, you know, which might have come down from old Salem times, and Cotton Mather tells even stranger things. You know how damned life-like Pickman's paintings were—how we all wondered where he got those faces.

Well—that paper wasn't a photograph of any background, after all. What it shewed was simply the monstrous being he was painting on that awful canvas. It was the model he was using—and its background was merely the wall of the cellar studio in minute detail. But by God, Eliot, *it was a photograph from life.*

Cool Air

You ask me to explain why I am afraid of a draught of cool air; why I shiver more than others upon entering a cold room, and seem nauseated and repelled when the chill of evening creeps through the heat of a mild autumn day. There are those who say I respond to cold as others do to a bad odour, and I am the last to deny the impression. What I will do is to relate the most horrible circumstance I ever encountered, and leave it to you to judge whether or not this forms a suitable explanation of my peculiarity.

It is a mistake to fancy that horror is associated inextricably with darkness, silence, and solitude. I found it in the glare of mid-afternoon, in the clangour of a metropolis, and in the teeming midst of a shabby and commonplace rooming-house with a prosaic landlady and two stalwart men by my side. In the spring of 1923 I had secured some dreary and unprofitable magazine work in the city of New York; and being unable to pay any substantial rent, began drifting from one cheap boarding establishment to another in search of a room which might combine the qualities of decent cleanliness, endurable furnishings, and very reasonable price. It soon developed that I had only a choice between different evils, but after a time I came upon a house in West Fourteenth Street which disgusted me much less than the others I had sampled.

The place was a four-story mansion of brownstone, dating apparently from the late forties, and fitted with woodwork and marble whose stained and sullied splendour argued a descent from high levels of tasteful opulence. In the rooms, large and lofty, and decorated with impossible paper and ridiculously ornate stucco cornices, there lingered a depressing mustiness and hint of obscure cookery; but the floors were clean, the linen tolerably regular, and the hot water not too often cold or turned off, so that I came to regard it as at least a bearable place to hibernate till one might really live again. The landlady, a slatternly, almost bearded Spanish woman named Herrero, did not annoy me with gossip or with criticisms of the late-burning electric light in my third-floor front hall room; and my fellow-lodgers were as quiet and uncommunicative as one might desire, being mostly Spaniards a little above the coarsest and crudest grade. Only the din of street cars in the thoroughfare below proved a serious annoyance.

I had been there about three weeks when the first odd incident occurred. One evening at about eight I heard a spattering on the floor and became suddenly aware that I had been smelling the pungent odour of ammonia for some time. Looking about, I saw that the ceiling was wet and dripping; the soaking apparently proceeding from a corner on the side toward the street. Anxious to stop the matter at its source, I hastened to the basement to tell the landlady; and was assured by her that the trouble would quickly be set right.

"Doctair Muñoz," she cried as she rushed upstairs ahead of me, "he have speel hees chemicals. He ees too seeck for doctair heemself—seecker and seecker all the time—but he weel not have no othair for help. He ees vairy queer in hees seeckness—all day he take funnee-smelling baths, and he cannot get excite or warm. All hees own housework he do—hees leetle room are full of bottles and machines, and he do not work as doctair. But he was great once—my fathair in Barcelona have hear of heem—and only joost now he feex a arm of the plumber that get hurt of sudden. He nevair go out, only on roof, and my boy Esteban he breeng heem hees food and laundry and mediceens and chemicals. My Gawd, the sal-ammoniac that man use for keep heem cool!"

Mrs. Herrero disappeared up the staircase to the fourth floor, and I returned to my room. The ammonia ceased to drip, and as I cleaned up what had spilled and opened the window for air, I heard the landlady's heavy footsteps above me. Dr. Muñoz I had never heard, save for certain sounds as of some gasoline-driven mechanism; since his step was soft and gentle. I wondered for a moment what the strange affliction of this man might be, and whether his obstinate refusal of outside aid were not the result of a rather baseless eccentricity. There is, I reflected tritely, an infinite deal of pathos in the state of an eminent person who has come down in the world.

I might never have known Dr. Muñoz had it not been for the heart attack that suddenly seized me one forenoon as I sat writing in my room. Physicians had told me of the danger of those spells, and I knew there was no time to be lost; so remembering what the landlady had said about the invalid's help of the injured workman, I dragged myself upstairs and knocked feebly at the door above mine. My knock was answered in good English by a curious voice some distance to the right, asking my name and business; and these things being stated, there came an opening of the door next to the one I had sought.

A rush of cool air greeted me; and though the day was one of the hottest of late June, I shivered as I crossed the threshold into a large apartment whose rich and tasteful decoration surprised me in this nest of squalor and seediness. A folding couch now filled its diurnal role of sofa, and the mahogany furniture, sumptuous hangings, old paintings, and mellow bookshelves all bespoke a gentleman's study rather than a boarding-house bedroom. I now saw that the hall room above mine—the "leetle room" of bottles and machines which Mrs. Herrero had mentioned—was merely the laboratory of the doctor; and that his main living quarters lay in the spacious adjoining room whose convenient alcoves and large contiguous bathroom permitted him to hide all dressers and obtrusive utilitarian devices. Dr. Muñoz, most certainly, was a man of birth, cultivation, and discrimination.

The figure before me was short but exquisitely proportioned, and clad in somewhat formal dress of perfect cut and fit. A high-bred face of masterful though not arrogant expression was adorned by a short iron-grey full beard, and an old-fashioned pince-nez shielded the full, dark eyes and surmounted an aquiline nose which gave a Moorish touch to a physiognomy otherwise dominantly Celtiberian. Thick, well-trimmed hair that argued the punctual calls of a barber was parted gracefully above a high forehead; and the whole picture was one of striking intelligence and superior blood and breeding.

Nevertheless, as I saw Dr. Muñoz in that blast of cool air, I felt a repugnance which nothing in his aspect could justify. Only his lividly inclined complexion and coldness of touch could have afforded a physical basis for this feeling, and even these things should have been excusable considering the man's known invalidism. It might, too, have been the singular cold that alienated me; for such chilliness was abnormal on so hot a day, and the abnormal always excites aversion, distrust, and fear.

But repugnance was soon forgotten in admiration, for the strange physician's extreme skill at once became manifest despite the ice-coldness and shakiness of his bloodless-looking hands. He clearly understood my needs at a glance, and ministered to them with a master's deftness; the while reassuring me in a finely modulated though oddly hollow and timbreless voice that he was the bitterest of sworn enemies to death, and had sunk his fortune and lost all his friends in a lifetime of bizarre experiment devoted to its bafflement and extirpation. Something of the benevolent fanatic seemed to reside in him, and he rambled on almost garrulously as he sounded my chest and mixed a suitable draught of drugs fetched from the smaller laboratory room. Evidently he found the society of a well-born man a rare novelty in this dingy environment, and was moved to unaccustomed speech as memories of better days surged over him.

His voice, if queer, was at least soothing; and I could not even perceive that he breathed as the fluent sentences rolled urbanely out. He sought to distract my mind from my own seizure by speaking of his theories and experiments; and I remember his tactfully consoling me about my weak heart by insisting that will and consciousness are stronger than organic life itself, so that if a bodily frame be but originally healthy and carefully preserved, it may through a scientific enhancement of these qualities retain a kind of nervous animation despite the most serious impairments, defects, or even absences in the battery of specific organs. He might, he half jestingly said, some day teach me to live—or at least to possess some kind of conscious existence—without any heart at all! For his part, he was afflicted with a complication of maladies requiring a very exact regimen which included constant cold. Any marked rise in temperature might, if prolonged, affect him fatally; and the frigidity of his habitation— some 55 or 56 degrees Fahrenheit—was maintained by an absorption system of ammonia cooling, the gasoline engine of whose pumps I had often heard in my own room below.

Relieved of my seizure in a marvellously short while, I left the shivery place a disciple and devotee of the gifted recluse. After that I paid him frequent overcoated calls; listening while he told of secret researches and almost ghastly results, and trembling a bit when I examined the unconventional and astonishingly ancient volumes on his shelves. I was eventually, I may add, almost cured of my disease for all time by his skilful ministrations. It seems that he did not scorn the incantations of the mediaevalists, since he believed these cryptic formulae to contain rare psychological stimuli which might conceivably have singular effects on the substance of a nervous system from which organic pulsations had fled. I was touched by his account of the aged Dr. Torres of Valencia, who had shared his earlier experiments with him through the great illness of eighteen years before, whence his present disorders proceeded. No sooner had the venerable practitioner saved his colleague than he himself succumbed to the grim enemy he had fought. Perhaps the strain had been too great; for Dr. Muñoz made it whisperingly clear—though not in detail—that the methods of healing had been most extraordinary, involving scenes and processes not welcomed by elderly and conservative Galens.

As the weeks passed, I observed with regret that my new friend was indeed slowly but unmistakably losing ground physically, as Mrs. Herrero had suggested. The livid aspect of his countenance was intensified, his voice became more hollow and indistinct, his muscular motions were less perfectly coordinated, and his mind and will displayed less resilience and initiative. Of this sad change he seemed by no means unaware, and little by little his expression and conversation both took on a gruesome irony which restored in me something of the subtle repulsion I had originally felt.

He developed strange caprices, acquiring a fondness for exotic spices and Egyptian incense till his room smelled like the vault of a sepulchred Pharaoh in the Valley of Kings. At the same time his demands for cold air increased, and with my aid he amplified the ammonia piping of his room and modified the pumps and feed of his refrigerating machine till he could keep the temperature as low as 34° or 40° and finally even 28°; the bathroom and laboratory, of course, being less chilled, in order that water might not freeze, and that chemical processes might not be impeded. The tenant adjoining him complained of the icy air from around the connecting door, so I helped him fit heavy hangings to obviate the difficulty. A kind of growing horror, of outré and morbid cast, seemed to possess him. He talked of death incessantly, but laughed hollowly when such things as burial or funeral arrangements were gently suggested.

All in all, he became a disconcerting and even gruesome companion; yet in my gratitude for his healing I could not well abandon him to the strangers around him, and was careful to dust his room and attend to his needs each day, muffled in a heavy ulster which I bought especially for the purpose. I likewise did much of his shopping, and gasped in bafflement at some of the chemicals he ordered from druggists and laboratory supply houses.

An increasing and unexplained atmosphere of panic seemed to rise around his apartment. The whole house, as I have said, had a musty odour; but the smell in his room was worse—and in spite of all the spices and incense, and the pungent chemicals of the now incessant baths which he insisted on taking unaided. I perceived that it must be connected with his ailment, and shuddered when I reflected on what that ailment might be. Mrs. Herrero crossed herself when she looked at him, and gave him up unreservedly to me; not even letting her son Esteban continue to run errands for him. When I suggested other physicians, the sufferer would fly into as much of a rage as he seemed to dare to entertain. He evidently feared the physical effect of violent emotion, yet his will and driving force waxed rather than waned, and he refused to be confined to his bed. The lassitude of his earlier ill days gave place to a return of his fiery purpose, so that he seemed about to hurl defiance at the death-daemon even as that ancient enemy seized him. The pretence of eating, always curiously like a formality with him, he virtually abandoned; and mental power alone appeared to keep him from total collapse.

He acquired a habit of writing long documents of some sort, which he carefully sealed and filled with injunctions that I transmit them after his death to certain persons whom he named—for the most part lettered East Indians, but including a once celebrated French physician now generally thought dead, and about whom the most inconceivable things had been whispered. As it happened, I burned all these papers undelivered and unopened. His aspect and voice became utterly frightful, and his presence almost unbearable. One September day an unexpected glimpse of him induced an epileptic fit in a man who had come to repair his electric desk lamp; a fit for which he prescribed effectively whilst keeping himself well out of sight. That man, oddly enough, had been through the terrors of the Great War without having incurred any fright so thorough.

Then, in the middle of October, the horror of horrors came with stupefying suddenness. One night about eleven the pump of the refrigerating machine broke down, so that within three hours the process of ammonia cooling became impossible. Dr. Muñoz summoned me by thumping on the floor, and I worked desperately to repair the injury while my host cursed in a tone whose lifeless, rattling hollowness surpassed description. My amateur efforts, however, proved of no use; and when I had brought in a mechanic from a neighbouring all-night garage we learned that nothing could be done till morning, when a new piston would have to be obtained. The moribund hermit's rage and fear, swelling to grotesque proportions, seemed likely to shatter what remained of his failing physique; and once a spasm caused him to clap his hands to his eyes and rush into the bathroom. He groped his way out with face tightly bandaged, and I never saw his eyes again.

The frigidity of the apartment was now sensibly diminishing, and at about 5 a.m. the doctor retired to the bathroom, commanding me to keep him supplied with all the ice I could obtain at all-night drug stores and cafeterias. As I would return from my sometimes discouraging trips and lay my spoils before the closed bathroom door, I could hear a restless splashing within, and a thick voice croaking out the order for "More—more!" At length a warm day broke, and the shops opened one by one. I asked Esteban either to help with the ice-fetching whilst I obtained the pump piston, or to order the piston while I continued with the ice; but instructed by his mother, he absolutely refused.

Finally I hired a seedy-looking loafer whom I encountered on the corner of Eighth Avenue to keep the patient supplied with ice from a little shop where I introduced him, and applied myself diligently to the task of finding a pump piston and engaging workmen competent to install it. The task seemed interminable, and I raged almost as violently as the hermit when I saw the hours slipping by in a breathless, foodless round of vain telephoning, and a hectic quest from place to place, hither and thither by subway and surface car. About noon I encountered a suitable supply house far downtown, and at approximately 1:30 p.m. arrived at my boarding-place with the necessary paraphernalia and two sturdy and intelligent mechanics. I had done all I could, and hoped I was in time.

Black terror, however, had preceded me. The house was in utter turmoil, and above the chatter of awed voices I heard a man praying in a deep basso. Fiendish things were in the air, and lodgers told over the beads of their rosaries as they caught the odour from beneath the doctor's closed door. The lounger I had hired, it seems, had fled screaming and mad-eyed not long after his second delivery of ice; perhaps as a result of excessive curiosity. He could not, of course, have locked the door behind him; yet it was now fastened, presumably from the inside. There was no sound within save a nameless sort of slow, thick dripping.

Briefly consulting with Mrs. Herrero and the workmen despite a fear that gnawed my inmost soul, I advised the breaking down of the door; but the landlady found a way to turn the key from the outside with some wire device. We had previously opened the doors of all the other rooms on that hall, and flung all the windows to the very top. Now, noses protected by handkerchiefs, we tremblingly invaded the accursed south room which blazed with the warm sun of early afternoon.

A kind of dark, slimy trail led from the open bathroom door to the hall door, and thence to the desk, where a terrible little pool had accumulated. Something was scrawled there in pencil in an awful, blind hand on a piece of paper hideously smeared as though by the very claws that traced the hurried last words. Then the trail led to the couch and ended unutterably.

What was, or had been, on the couch I cannot and dare not say here. But this is what I shiveringly puzzled out on the stickily smeared paper before I drew a match and burned it to a crisp; what I puzzled out in terror as the landlady and two mechanics rushed frantically from that hellish place to babble their incoherent stories at the nearest police station. The nauseous words seemed well-nigh incredible in that yellow sunlight, with the clatter of cars and motor trucks ascending clamorously from crowded Fourteenth Street, yet I confess that I believed them then. Whether I believe them now I honestly do not know. There are things about which it is better not to speculate, and all that I can say is that I hate the smell of ammonia, and grow faint at a draught of unusually cool air.

"The end," ran that noisome scrawl, "is here. No more ice—the man looked and ran away. Warmer every minute, and the tissues can't last. I fancy you know—what I said about the will and the nerves and the preserved body after the organs ceased to work. It was good theory, but couldn't keep up indefinitely. There was a gradual deterioration I had not foreseen. Dr. Torres knew, but the shock killed him. He couldn't stand what he had to do—he had to get me in a strange, dark place when he minded my letter and nursed me back. And the organs never would work again. It had to be done my way—artificial preservation—*for you see I died that time eighteen years ago.*"

The Thing on the Doorstep

I.

It is true that I have sent six bullets through the head of my best friend, and yet I hope to shew by this statement that I am not his murderer. At first I shall be called a madman—madder than the man I shot in his cell at the Arkham Sanitarium. Later some of my readers will weigh each statement, correlate it with the known facts, and ask themselves how I could have believed otherwise than as I did after facing the evidence of that horror—that thing on the doorstep.

Until then I also saw nothing but madness in the wild tales I have acted on. Even now I ask myself whether I was misled—or whether I am not mad after all. I do not know—but others have strange things to tell of Edward and Asenath Derby, and even the stolid police are at their wits' ends to account for that last terrible visit. They have tried weakly to concoct a theory of a ghastly jest or warning by discharged servants, yet they know in their hearts that the truth is something infinitely more terrible and incredible.

So I say that I have not murdered Edward Derby. Rather have I avenged him, and in so doing purged the earth of a horror whose survival might have loosed untold terrors on all mankind. There are black zones of shadow close to our daily paths, and now and then some evil soul breaks a passage through. When that happens, the man who knows must strike before reckoning the consequences.

I have known Edward Pickman Derby all his life. Eight years my junior, he was so precocious that we had much in common from the time he was eight and I sixteen. He was the most phenomenal child scholar I have ever known, and at seven was writing verse of a sombre, fantastic, almost morbid cast which astonished the tutors surrounding him. Perhaps his private education and coddled seclusion had something to do with his premature flowering. An only child, he had organic weaknesses which startled his doting parents and caused them to keep him closely chained to their side. He was never allowed out without his nurse, and seldom had a chance to play unconstrainedly with other children. All this doubtless fostered a strange, secretive inner life in the boy, with imagination as his one avenue of freedom.

At any rate, his juvenile learning was prodigious and bizarre; and his facile writings such as to captivate me despite my greater age.

About that time I had leanings toward art of a somewhat grotesque cast, and I found in this younger child a rare kindred spirit. What lay behind our joint love of shadows and marvels was, no doubt, the ancient, mouldering, and subtly fearsome town in which we lived—witch-cursed, legend-haunted Arkham, whose huddled, sagging gambrel roofs and crumbling Georgian balustrades brood out the centuries beside the darkly muttering Miskatonic.

As time went by I turned to architecture and gave up my design of illustrating a book of Edward's daemoniac poems, yet our comradeship suffered no lessening. Young Derby's odd genius developed remarkably, and in his eighteenth year his collected nightmare-lyrics made a real sensation when issued under the title *Azathoth and Other Horrors*. He was a close correspondent of the notorious Baudelairean poet Justin Geoffrey, who wrote *The People of the Monolith* and died screaming in a madhouse in 1926 after a visit to a sinister, ill-regarded village in Hungary.

In self-reliance and practical affairs, however, Derby was greatly retarded because of his coddled existence. His health had improved, but his habits of childish dependence were fostered by overcareful parents; so that he never travelled alone, made independent decisions, or assumed responsibilities. It was early seen that he would not be equal to a struggle in the business or professional arena, but the family fortune was so ample that this formed no tragedy. As he grew to years of manhood he retained a deceptive aspect of boyishness. Blond and blue-eyed, he had the fresh complexion of a child; and his attempts to raise a moustache were discernible only with difficulty. His voice was soft and light, and his pampered, unexercised life gave him a juvenile chubbiness rather than the paunchiness of premature middle age. He was of good height, and his handsome face would have made him a notable gallant had not his shyness held him to seclusion and bookishness.

Derby's parents took him abroad every summer, and he was quick to seize on the surface aspects of European thought and expression. His Poe-like talents turned more and more toward the decadent, and other artistic sensitivenesses and yearnings were half-aroused in him. We had great discussions in those days. I had been through Harvard, had studied in a Boston architect's office, had married, and had finally returned to Arkham to practice my profession—settling in the family homestead in Saltonstall St. since my father had moved to Florida for his health. Edward used to call almost every evening, till I came to regard him as one of the household. He had a characteristic way of ringing the doorbell or sounding the knocker that grew to be a veritable code signal, so that after dinner I always listened for the familiar three brisk strokes followed by two more after a pause. Less frequently I would visit at his house and note with envy the obscure volumes in his constantly growing library.

Derby went through Miskatonic University in Arkham, since his parents would not let him board away from them. He entered at sixteen and completed his course in three years, majoring in English and French literature and receiving high marks in everything but mathematics and the sciences. He mingled very little with the other students, though looking enviously at the "daring" or "Bohemian" set—whose superficially "smart" language and meaninglessly ironic pose he aped, and whose dubious conduct he wished he dared adopt.

What he did do was to become an almost fanatical devotee of subterranean magical lore, for which Miskatonic's library was and is famous. Always a dweller on the surface of phantasy and strangeness, he now delved deep into the actual runes and riddles left by a fabulous past for the guidance or puzzlement of posterity. He read things like the frightful *Book of Eibon*, the *Unaussprechlichen Kulten* of von Junzt, and the forbidden *Necronomicon* of the mad Arab Abdul Alhazred, though he did not tell his parents he had seen them. Edward was twenty when my son and only child was born, and seemed pleased when I named the newcomer Edward Derby Upton, after him.

By the time he was twenty-five Edward Derby was a prodigiously learned man and a fairly well-known poet and fantaisiste, though his lack of contacts and responsibilities had slowed down his literary growth by making his products derivative and overbookish. I was perhaps his closest friend—finding him an inexhaustible mine of vital theoretical topics, while he relied on me for advice in whatever matters he did not wish to refer to his parents. He remained single—more through shyness, inertia, and parental protectiveness than through inclination—and moved in society only to the slightest and most perfunctory extent. When the war came both health and ingrained timidity kept him at home. I went to Plattsburg for a commission, but never got overseas.

So the years wore on. Edward's mother died when he was thirty-four, and for months he was incapacitated by some odd psychological malady. His father took him to Europe, however, and he managed to pull out of his trouble without visible effects. Afterward he seemed to feel a sort of grotesque exhilaration, as if of partial escape from some unseen bondage. He began to mingle in the more "advanced" college set despite his middle age, and was present at some extremely wild doings—on one occasion paying heavy blackmail (which he borrowed of me) to keep his presence at a certain affair from his father's notice. Some of the whispered rumours about the wild Miskatonic set were extremely singular. There was even talk of black magic and of happenings utterly beyond credibility.

II.

Edward was thirty-eight when he met Asenath Waite. She was, I judge, about twenty-three at the time; and was taking a special course in mediaeval metaphysics at Miskatonic. The daughter of a friend of mine had met her before—in the Hall School at Kingsport—and had been inclined to shun her because of her odd reputation. She was dark, smallish, and very good-looking except for overprotuberant eyes; but something in her expression alienated extremely sensitive people. It was, however, largely her origin and conversation which caused average folk to avoid her. She was one of the Innsmouth Waites, and dark legends have clustered for generations about crumbling, half-deserted Innsmouth and its people. There are tales of horrible bargains about the year 1850, and of a strange element "not quite human" in the ancient families of the run-down fishing port— tales such as only old-time Yankees can devise and repeat with proper awesomeness.

Asenath's case was aggravated by the fact that she was Ephraim Waite's daughter—the child of his old age by an unknown wife who always went veiled. Ephraim lived in a half-decayed mansion in Washington Street, Innsmouth, and those who had seen the place (Arkham folk avoid going to Innsmouth whenever they can) declared that the attic windows were always boarded, and that strange sounds sometimes floated from within as evening drew on. The old man was known to have been a prodigious magical student in his day, and legend averred that he could raise or quell storms at sea according to his whim. I had seen him once or twice in my youth as he came to Arkham to consult forbidden tomes at the college library, and had hated his wolfish, saturnine face with its tangle of iron-grey beard. He had died insane—under rather queer circumstances—just before his daughter (by his will made a nominal ward of the principal) entered the Hall School, but she had been his morbidly avid pupil and looked fiendishly like him at times.

The friend whose daughter had gone to school with Asenath Waite repeated many curious things when the news of Edward's acquaintance with her began to spread about. Asenath, it seemed, had posed as a kind of magician at school; and had really seemed able to accomplish some highly baffling marvels. She professed to be able to raise thunderstorms, though her seeming success was generally laid to some uncanny knack at prediction. All animals markedly disliked her, and she could make any dog howl by certain motions of her right hand. There were times when she displayed snatches of knowledge and language very singular—and very shocking—for a young girl; when she would frighten her schoolmates with leers and winks of an inexplicable kind, and would seem to extract an obscene and zestful irony from her present situation.

Most unusual, though, were the well-attested cases of her influence over other persons. She was, beyond question, a genuine hypnotist. By gazing peculiarly at a fellow-student she would often give the latter a distinct feeling of *exchanged personality*—as if the subject were placed momentarily in the magician's body and able to stare half across the room at her real body, whose eyes blazed and protruded with an alien expression. Asenath often made wild claims about the nature of consciousness and about its independence of the physical frame—or at least from the life-processes of the physical frame. Her crowning rage, however, was that she was not a man; since she believed a male brain had certain unique and far-reaching cosmic powers. Given a man's brain, she declared, she could not only equal but surpass her father in mastery of unknown forces.

Edward met Asenath at a gathering of "intelligentsia" held in one of the students' rooms, and could talk of nothing else when he came to see me the next day. He had found her full of the interests and erudition which engrossed him most, and was in addition wildly taken with her appearance. I had never seen the young woman, and recalled casual references only faintly, but I knew who she was. It seemed rather regrettable that Derby should become so upheaved about her; but I said nothing to discourage him, since infatuation thrives on opposition. He was not, he said, mentioning her to his father.

In the next few weeks I heard of very little but Asenath from young Derby. Others now remarked Edward's autumnal gallantry, though they agreed that he did not look even nearly his actual age, or seem at all inappropriate as an escort for his bizarre divinity. He was only a trifle paunchy despite his indolence and self-indulgence, and his face was absolutely without lines. Asenath, on the other hand, had the premature crow's feet which come from the exercise of an intense will.

About this time Edward brought the girl to call on me, and I at once saw that his interest was by no means one-sided. She eyed him continually with an almost predatory air, and I perceived that their intimacy was beyond untangling. Soon afterward I had a visit from old Mr. Derby, whom I had always admired and respected. He had heard the tales of his son's new friendship, and had wormed the whole truth out of "the boy." Edward meant to marry Asenath, and had even been looking at houses in the suburbs. Knowing my usually great influence with his son, the father wondered if I could help to break the ill-advised affair off; but I regretfully expressed my doubts. This time it was not a question of Edward's weak will but of the woman's strong will. The perennial child had transferred his dependence from the parental image to a new and stronger image, and nothing could be done about it.

The wedding was performed a month later—by a justice of the peace, according to the bride's request. Mr. Derby, at my advice, offered no opposition; and he, my wife, my son, and I attended the brief ceremony—the other guests being wild young people from the college. Asenath had bought the old Crowninshield place in the country at the end of High Street, and they proposed to settle there after a short trip to Innsmouth, whence three servants and some books and household goods were to be brought. It was probably not so much consideration for Edward and his father as a personal wish to be near the college, its library, and its crowd of "sophisticates", that made Asenath settle in Arkham instead of returning permanently home.

When Edward called on me after the honeymoon I thought he looked slightly changed. Asenath had made him get rid of the undeveloped moustache, but there was more than that. He looked soberer and more thoughtful, his habitual pout of childish rebelliousness being exchanged for a look almost of genuine sadness. I was puzzled to decide whether I liked or disliked the change. Certainly, he seemed for the moment more normally adult than ever before. Perhaps the marriage was a good thing—might not the change of dependence form a start toward actual *neutralisation*, leading ultimately to responsible independence? He came alone, for Asenath was very busy. She had brought a vast store of books and apparatus from Innsmouth (Derby shuddered as he spoke the name), and was finishing the restoration of the Crowninshield house and grounds.

Her home in—that town—was a rather disquieting place, but certain objects in it had taught him some surprising things. He was progressing fast in esoteric lore now that he had Asenath's guidance. Some of the experiments she proposed were very daring and radical—he did not feel at liberty to describe them—but he had confidence in her powers and intentions. The three servants were very queer—an incredibly aged couple who had been with old Ephraim and referred occasionally to him and to Asenath's dead mother in a cryptic way, and a swarthy young wench who had marked anomalies of feature and seemed to exude a perpetual odour of fish.

III.

For the next two years I saw less and less of Derby. A fortnight would sometimes slip by without the familiar three-and-two strokes at the front door; and when he did call—or when, as happened with increasing infrequency, I called on him—he was very little disposed to converse on vital topics. He had become secretive about those occult studies which he used to describe and discuss so minutely, and preferred not to talk of his wife. She had aged tremendously since her marriage, till now—oddly enough—she seemed the elder of the two. Her face held the most concentratedly determined expression I had ever seen, and her whole aspect seemed to gain a vague, unplaceable repulsiveness. My wife and son noticed it as much as I, and we all ceased gradually to call on her—for which, Edward admitted in one of his boyishly tactless moments, she was unmitigatedly grateful. Occasionally the Derbys would go on long trips—ostensibly to Europe, though Edward sometimes hinted at obscurer destinations.

It was after the first year that people began talking about the change in Edward Derby. It was very casual talk, for the change was purely psychological; but it brought up some interesting points. Now and then, it seemed, Edward was observed to wear an expression and to do things wholly incompatible with his usual flabby nature. For example—although in the old days he could not drive a car, he was now seen occasionally to dash into or out of the old Crowninshield driveway with Asenath's powerful Packard, handling it like a master, and meeting traffic entanglements with a skill and determination utterly alien to his accustomed nature. In such cases he seemed always to be just back from some trip or just starting on one—what sort of trip, no one could guess, although he mostly favoured the Innsmouth road.

Oddly, the metamorphosis did not seem altogether pleasing. People said he looked too much like his wife, or like old Ephraim Waite himself, in these moments—or perhaps these moments seemed unnatural because they were so rare. Sometimes, hours after starting out in this way, he would return listlessly sprawled on the rear seat of the car while an obviously hired chauffeur or mechanic drove. Also, his preponderant aspect on the streets during his decreasing round of social contacts (including, I may say, his calls on me) was the old-time indecisive one—its irresponsible childishness even more marked than in the past. While Asenath's face aged, Edward's—aside from those exceptional occasions—actually relaxed into a kind of exaggerated immaturity, save when a trace of the new sadness or understanding would flash across it. It was really very puzzling. Meanwhile the Derbys almost dropped out of the gay college circle—not through their own disgust, we heard, but because something about their present studies shocked even the most callous of the other decadents.

It was in the third year of the marriage that Edward began to hint openly to me of a certain fear and dissatisfaction. He would let fall remarks about things 'going too far', and would talk darkly about the need of 'saving his identity'. At first I ignored such references, but in time I began to question him guardedly, remembering what my friend's daughter had said about Asenath's hypnotic influence over the other girls at school—the cases where students had thought they were in her body looking across the room at themselves. This questioning seemed to make him at once alarmed and grateful, and once he mumbled something about having a serious talk with me later.

About this time old Mr. Derby died, for which I was afterward very thankful. Edward was badly upset, though by no means disorganised. He had seen astonishingly little of his parent since his marriage, for Asenath had concentrated in herself all his vital sense of family linkage. Some called him callous in his loss—especially since those jaunty and confident moods in the car began to increase. He now wished to move back into the old Derby mansion, but Asenath insisted on staying in the Crowninshield house, to which she had become well adjusted.

Not long afterward my wife heard a curious thing from a friend—one of the few who had not dropped the Derbys. She had been out to the end of High St. to call on the couple, and had seen a car shoot briskly out of the drive with Edward's oddly confident and almost sneering face above the wheel. Ringing the bell, she had been told by the repulsive wench that Asenath was also out; but had chanced to look up at the house in leaving. There, at one of Edward's library windows, she had glimpsed a hastily withdrawn face—a face whose expression of pain, defeat, and wistful hopelessness was poignant beyond description. It was—incredibly enough in view of its usual domineering cast—Asenath's; yet the caller had vowed that in that instant the sad, muddled eyes of poor Edward were gazing out from it.

Edward's calls now grew a trifle more frequent, and his hints occasionally became concrete. What he said was not to be believed, even in centuried and legend-haunted Arkham; but he threw out his dark lore with a sincerity and convincingness which made one fear for his sanity. He talked about terrible meetings in lonely places, of Cyclopean ruins in the heart of the Maine woods beneath which vast staircases lead down to abysses of nighted secrets, of complex angles that lead through invisible walls to other regions of space and time, and of hideous exchanges of personality that permitted explorations in remote and forbidden places, on other worlds, and in different space-time continua.

He would now and then back up certain crazy hints by exhibiting objects which utterly nonplussed me—elusively coloured and bafflingly textured objects like nothing ever heard of on earth, whose insane curves and surfaces answered no conceivable purpose and followed no conceivable geometry. These things, he said, came 'from outside'; and his wife knew how to get them. Sometimes—but always in frightened and ambiguous whispers—he would suggest things about old Ephraim Waite, whom he had seen occasionally at the college library in the old days. These adumbrations were never specific, but seemed to revolve around some especially horrible doubt as to whether the old wizard were really dead—in a spiritual as well as corporeal sense.

At times Derby would halt abruptly in his revelations, and I wondered whether Asenath could possibly have divined his speech at a distance and cut him off through some unknown sort of telepathic mesmerism—some power of the kind she had displayed at school. Certainly, she suspected that he told me things, for as the weeks passed she tried to stop his visits with words and glances of a most inexplicable potency. Only with difficulty could he get to see me, for although he would pretend to be going somewhere else, some invisible force would generally clog his motions or make him forget his destination for the time being. His visits usually came when Asenath was away—'away in her own body,' as he once oddly put it. She always found out later—the servants watched his goings and comings—but evidently she thought it inexpedient to do anything drastic.

IV.

Derby had been married more than three years on that August day when I got the telegram from Maine. I had not seen him for two months, but had heard he was away "on business." Asenath was supposed to be with him, though watchful gossips declared there was someone upstairs in the house behind the doubly curtained windows. They had watched the purchases made by the servants. And now the town marshal of Chesuncook had wired of the draggled madman who stumbled out of the woods with delirious ravings and screamed to me for protection. It was Edward—and he had been just able to recall his own name and my name and address.

Chesuncook is close to the wildest, deepest, and least explored forest belt in Maine, and it took a whole day of feverish jolting through fantastic and forbidding scenery to get there in a car. I found Derby in a cell at the town farm, vacillating between frenzy and apathy. He knew me at once, and began pouring out a meaningless, half-incoherent torrent of words in my direction.

"Dan—for God's sake! The pit of the shoggoths! Down the six thousand steps ... the abomination of abominations ... I never would let her take me, and then I found myself there. ... Iä! Shub-Niggurath! ... The shape rose up from the altar, and there were 500 that howled. ... The Hooded Thing bleated 'Kamog! Kamog!'—that was old Ephraim's secret name in the coven. ... I was there, where she promised she wouldn't take me. ... A minute before I was locked in the library, and then I was there where she had gone with my body—in the place of utter blasphemy, the unholy pit where the black realm begins and the watcher guards the gate. ... I saw a shoggoth—it changed shape. ... I can't stand it. ... I won't stand it. ... I'll kill her if she ever sends me there again. ... I'll kill that entity ... her, him, it ... I'll kill it! I'll kill it with my own hands!"

It took me an hour to quiet him, but he subsided at last. The next day I got him decent clothes in the village, and set out with him for Arkham. His fury of hysteria was spent, and he was inclined to be silent; though he began muttering darkly to himself when the car passed through Augusta—as if the sight of a city aroused unpleasant memories. It was clear that he did not wish to go home; and considering the fantastic delusions he seemed to have about his wife—delusions undoubtedly springing from some actual hypnotic ordeal to which he had been subjected—I thought it would be better if he did not. I would, I resolved, put him up myself for a time; no matter what unpleasantness it would make with Asenath. Later I would help him get a divorce, for most assuredly there were mental factors which made this marriage suicidal for him. When we struck open country again Derby's muttering faded away, and I let him nod and drowse on the seat beside me as I drove.

During our sunset dash through Portland the muttering commenced again, more distinctly than before, and as I listened I caught a stream of utterly insane drivel about Asenath. The extent to which she had preyed on Edward's nerves was plain, for he had woven a whole set of hallucinations around her. His present predicament, he mumbled furtively, was only one of a long series. She was getting hold of him, and he knew that some day she would never let go. Even now she probably let him go only when she had to, because she couldn't hold on long at a time. She constantly took his body and went to nameless places for nameless rites, leaving him in her body and locking him upstairs—but sometimes she couldn't hold on, and he would find himself suddenly in his own body again in some far-off, horrible, and perhaps unknown place. Sometimes she'd get hold of him again and sometimes she couldn't. Often he was left stranded somewhere as I had found him ... time and again he had to find his way home from frightful distances, getting somebody to drive the car after he found it.

The worst thing was that she was holding on to him longer and longer at a time. She wanted to be a man—to be fully human—that was why she got hold of him. She had sensed the mixture of fine-wrought brain and weak will in him. Some day she would crowd him out and disappear with his body—disappear to become a great magician like her father and leave him marooned in that female shell that wasn't even quite human. Yes, he knew about the Innsmouth blood now. There had been traffick with things from the sea—it was horrible. ... And old Ephraim—he had known the secret, and when he grew old did a hideous thing to keep alive ... he wanted to live forever ... demonstration had taken place already.

As Derby muttered on I turned to look at him closely, verifying the impression of change which an earlier scrutiny had given me. Paradoxically, he seemed in better shape than usual—harder, more normally developed, and without the trace of sickly flabbiness caused by his indolent habits. It was as if he had been really active and properly exercised for the first time in his coddled life, and I judged that Asenath's force must have pushed him into unwonted channels of motion and alertness. But just now his mind was in a pitiable state; for he was mumbling wild extravagances about his wife, about black magic, about old Ephraim, and about some revelation which would convince even me. He repeated names which I recognised from bygone browsings in forbidden volumes, and at times made me shudder with a certain thread of mythological consistency—of convincing coherence—which ran through his maundering. Again and again he would pause, as if to gather courage for some final and terrible disclosure.

"Dan, Dan, don't you remember him—the wild eyes and the unkempt beard that never turned white? He glared at me once, and I never forgot it. Now she glares that way. *And I know why!* He found it in the *Necronomicon*—the formula. I don't dare tell you the page yet, but when I do you can read and understand. Then you will know what has engulfed me. On, on, on, on—body to body to body—he means never to die. The life-glow—he knows how to break the link ... it can flicker on a while even when the body is dead. I'll give you hints, and maybe you'll guess. Listen, Dan—do you know why my wife always takes such pains with that silly backhand writing? Have you ever seen a manuscript of old Ephraim's? Do you want to know why I shivered when I saw some hasty notes Asenath had jotted down?

"Asenath ... *is there such a person?* Why did they half think there was poison in old Ephraim's stomach? Why do the Gilmans whisper about the way he shrieked—like a frightened child—when he went mad and Asenath locked him up in the padded attic room where—the other— had been? *Was it old Ephraim's soul that was locked in? Who locked in whom?* Why had he been looking for months for someone with a fine mind and a weak will? Why did he curse that his daughter wasn't a son? Tell me, Daniel Upton—*what devilish exchange was perpetrated in the house of horror where that blasphemous monster had his trusting, weak-willed, half-human child at his mercy?* Didn't he make it permanent—as she'll do in the end with me? Tell me why that thing that calls itself Asenath writes differently when off guard, *so that you can't tell its script from ...*"

Then the thing happened. Derby's voice was rising to a thin treble scream as he raved, when suddenly it was shut off with an almost mechanical click. I thought of those other occasions at my home when his confidences had abruptly ceased—when I had half fancied that some obscure telepathic wave of Asenath's mental force was intervening to keep him silent. This, though, was something altogether different—and, I felt, infinitely more horrible. The face beside me was twisted almost unrecognisably for a moment, while through the whole body there passed a shivering motion—as if all the bones, organs, muscles, nerves, and glands were readjusting themselves to a radically different posture, set of stresses, and general personality.

Just where the supreme horror lay, I could not for my life tell; yet there swept over me such a swamping wave of sickness and repulsion—such a freezing, petrifying sense of utter alienage and abnormality—that my grasp of the wheel grew feeble and uncertain. The figure beside me seemed less like a lifelong friend than like some monstrous intrusion from outer space—some damnable, utterly accursed focus of unknown and malign cosmic forces.

I had faltered only a moment, but before another moment was over my companion had seized the wheel and forced me to change places with him. The dusk was now very thick, and the lights of Portland far behind, so I could not see much of his face. The blaze of his eyes, though, was phenomenal; and I knew that he must now be in that queerly energised state—so unlike his usual self—which so many people had noticed. It seemed odd and incredible that listless Edward Derby—he who could never assert himself, and who had never learned to drive—should be ordering me about and taking the wheel of my own car, yet that was precisely what had happened. He did not speak for some time, and in my inexplicable horror I was glad he did not.

In the lights of Biddeford and Saco I saw his firmly set mouth, and shivered at the blaze of his eyes. The people were right—he did look damnably like his wife and like old Ephraim when in these moods. I did not wonder that the moods were disliked—there was certainly something unnatural and diabolic in them, and I felt the sinister element all the more because of the wild ravings I had been hearing. This man, for all my lifelong knowledge of Edward Pickman Derby, was a stranger—an intrusion of some sort from the black abyss.

He did not speak until we were on a dark stretch of road, and when he did his voice seemed utterly unfamiliar. It was deeper, firmer, and more decisive than I had ever known it to be; while its accent and pronunciation were altogether changed—though vaguely, remotely, and rather disturbingly recalling something I could not quite place. There was, I thought, a trace of very profound and very genuine irony in the timbre—not the flashy, meaninglessly jaunty pseudo-irony of the callow "sophisticate", which Derby had habitually affected, but something grim, basic, pervasive, and potentially evil. I marvelled at the self-possession so soon following the spell of panic-struck muttering.

"I hope you'll forget my attack back there, Upton," he was saying. "You know what my nerves are, and I guess you can excuse such things. I'm enormously grateful, of course, for this lift home.

"And you must forget, too, any crazy things I may have been saying about my wife—and about things in general. That's what comes from overstudy in a field like mine. My philosophy is full of bizarre concepts, and when the mind gets worn out it cooks up all sorts of imaginary concrete applications. I shall take a rest from now on—you probably won't see me for some time, and you needn't blame Asenath for it.

"This trip was a bit queer, but it's really very simple. There are certain Indian relics in the north woods—standing stones, and all that—which mean a good deal in folklore, and Asenath and I are following that stuff up. It was a hard search, so I seem to have gone off my head. I must send somebody for the car when I get home. A month's relaxation will put me back on my feet."

I do not recall just what my own part of the conversation was, for the baffling alienage of my seatmate filled all my consciousness. With every moment my feeling of elusive cosmic horror increased, till at length I was in a virtual delirium of longing for the end of the drive. Derby did not offer to relinquish the wheel, and I was glad of the speed with which Portsmouth and Newburyport flashed by.

At the junction where the main highway runs inland and avoids Innsmouth I was half afraid my driver would take the bleak shore road that goes through that damnable place. He did not, however, but darted rapidly past Rowley and Ipswich toward our destination. We reached Arkham before midnight, and found the lights still on at the old Crowninshield house. Derby left the car with a hasty repetition of his thanks, and I drove home alone with a curious feeling of relief. It had been a terrible drive—all the more terrible because I could not quite tell why—and I did not regret Derby's forecast of a long absence from my company.

V.

The next two months were full of rumours. People spoke of seeing Derby more and more in his new energised state, and Asenath was scarcely ever in to her few callers. I had only one visit from Edward, when he called briefly in Asenath's car—duly reclaimed from wherever he had left it in Maine—to get some books he had lent me. He was in his new state, and paused only long enough for some evasively polite remarks. It was plain that he had nothing to discuss with me when in this condition—and I noticed that he did not even trouble to give the old three-and-two signal when ringing the doorbell. As on that evening in the car, I felt a faint, infinitely deep horror which I could not explain; so that his swift departure was a prodigious relief.

In mid-September Derby was away for a week, and some of the decadent college set talked knowingly of the matter—hinting at a meeting with a notorious cult-leader, lately expelled from England, who had established headquarters in New York. For my part I could not get that strange ride from Maine out of my head. The transformation I had witnessed had affected me profoundly, and I caught myself again and again trying to account for the thing—and for the extreme horror it had inspired in me.

But the oddest rumours were those about the sobbing in the old Crowninshield house. The voice seemed to be a woman's, and some of the younger people thought it sounded like Asenath's. It was heard only at rare intervals, and would sometimes be choked off as if by force. There was talk of an investigation, but this was dispelled one day when Asenath appeared in the streets and chatted in a sprightly way with a large number of acquaintances—apologising for her recent absences and speaking incidentally about the nervous breakdown and hysteria of a guest from Boston. The guest was never seen, but Asenath's appearance left nothing to be said. And then someone complicated matters by whispering that the sobs had once or twice been in a man's voice.

One evening in mid-October I heard the familiar three-and-two ring at the front door. Answering it myself, I found Edward on the steps, and saw in a moment that his personality was the old one which I had not encountered since the day of his ravings on that terrible ride from Chesuncook. His face was twitching with a mixture of odd emotions in which fear and triumph seemed to share dominion, and he looked furtively over his shoulder as I closed the door behind him.

Following me clumsily to the study, he asked for some whiskey to steady his nerves. I forbore to question him, but waited till he felt like beginning whatever he wanted to say. At length he ventured some information in a choking voice.

"Asenath has gone, Dan. We had a long talk last night while the servants were out, and I made her promise to stop preying on me. Of course I had certain—certain occult defences I never told you about. She had to give in, but got frightfully angry. Just packed up and started for New York—walked right out to catch the 8:20 in to Boston. I suppose people will talk, but I can't help that. You needn't mention that there was any trouble—just say she's gone on a long research trip.

"She's probably going to stay with one of her horrible groups of devotees. I hope she'll go west and get a divorce—anyhow, I've made her promise to keep away and let me alone. It was horrible, Dan—she was stealing my body—crowding me out—making a prisoner of me. I laid low and pretended to let her do it, but I had to be on the watch. I could plan if I was careful, for she can't read my mind literally, or in detail. All she could read of my planning was a sort of general mood of rebellion—and she always thought I was helpless. Never thought I could get the best of her ... but I had a spell or two that worked."

Derby looked over his shoulder and took some more whiskey.

"I paid off those damned servants this morning when they got back. They were ugly about it, and asked questions, but they went. They're her kind—Innsmouth people—and were hand and glove with her. I hope they'll let me alone—I didn't like the way they laughed when they walked away. I must get as many of Dad's old servants again as I can. I'll move back home now.

"I suppose you think I'm crazy, Dan—but Arkham history ought to hint at things that back up what I've told you—and what I'm going to tell you. You've seen one of the changes, too—in your car after I told you about Asenath that day coming home from Maine. That was when she got me—drove me out of my body. The last thing of the ride I remember was when I was all worked up trying to tell you *what that she-devil is*. Then she got me, and in a flash I was back at the house—in the library where those damned servants had me locked up—and in that cursed fiend's body ... that isn't even human. ... You know, it was she you must have ridden home with ... that preying wolf in my body. ... You ought to have known the difference!"

I shuddered as Derby paused. Surely, I *had* known the difference—yet could I accept an explanation as insane as this? But my distracted caller was growing even wilder.

"I had to save myself—I had to, Dan! She'd have got me for good at Hallowmass—they hold a Sabbat up there beyond Chesuncook, and the sacrifice would have clinched things. She'd have got me for good ... she'd have been I, and I'd have been she ... forever ... too late. ... My body'd have been hers for good. ... She'd have been a man, and fully human, just as she wanted to be. ... I suppose she'd have put me out of the way—killed her own ex-body with me in it, damn her, *just as she did before*—just as she, he, or it did before ...."

Edward's face was now atrociously distorted, and he bent it uncomfortably close to mine as his voice fell to a whisper.

"You must know what I hinted in the car—*that she isn't Asenath at all, but really old Ephraim himself.* I suspected it a year and a half ago, but I know it now. Her handwriting shews it when she's off guard—sometimes she jots down a note in writing that's just like her father's manuscripts, stroke for stroke—and sometimes she says things that nobody but an old man like Ephraim could say. He changed forms with her when he felt death coming—she was the only one he could find with the right kind of brain and a weak enough will—he got her body permanently, just as she almost got mine, and then poisoned the old body he'd put her into. Haven't you seen old Ephraim's soul glaring out of that she-devil's eyes dozens of times ... and out of mine when she had control of my body?"

The whisperer was panting, and paused for breath. I said nothing, and when he resumed his voice was nearer normal. This, I reflected, was a case for the asylum, but I would not be the one to send him there. Perhaps time and freedom from Asenath would do its work. I could see that he would never wish to dabble in morbid occultism again.

"I'll tell you more later—I must have a long rest now. I'll tell you something of the forbidden horrors she led me into—something of the age-old horrors that even now are festering in out-of-the-way corners with a few monstrous priests to keep them alive. Some people know things about the universe that nobody ought to know, and can do things that nobody ought to be able to do. I've been in it up to my neck, but that's the end. Today I'd burn that damned *Necronomicon* and all the rest if I were librarian at Miskatonic.

"But she can't get me now. I must get out of that accursed house as soon as I can, and settle down at home. You'll help me, I know, if I need help. Those devilish servants, you know ... and if people should get too inquisitive about Asenath. You see, I can't give them her address. ... Then there are certain groups of searchers—certain cults, you know—that might misunderstand our breaking up ... some of them have damnably curious ideas and methods. I know you'll stand by me if anything happens—even if I have to tell you a lot that will shock you. ..."

I had Edward stay and sleep in one of the guest-chambers that night, and in the morning he seemed calmer. We discussed certain possible arrangements for his moving back into the Derby mansion, and I hoped he would lose no time in making the change. He did not call the next evening, but I saw him frequently during the ensuing weeks. We talked as little as possible about strange and unpleasant things, but discussed the renovation of the old Derby house, and the travels which Edward promised to take with my son and me the following summer.

Of Asenath we said almost nothing, for I saw that the subject was a peculiarly disturbing one. Gossip, of course, was rife; but that was no novelty in connexion with the strange ménage at the old Crowninshield house. One thing I did not like was what Derby's banker let fall in an overexpansive mood at the Miskatonic Club—about the cheques Edward was sending regularly to a Moses and Abigail Sargent and a Eunice Babson in Innsmouth. That looked as if those evil-faced servants were extorting some kind of tribute from him—yet he had not mentioned the matter to me.

I wished that the summer—and my son's Harvard vacation—would come, so that we could get Edward to Europe. He was not, I soon saw, mending as rapidly as I had hoped he would; for there was something a bit hysterical in his occasional exhilaration, while his moods of fright and depression were altogether too frequent. The old Derby house was ready by December, yet Edward constantly put off moving. Though he hated and seemed to fear the Crowninshield place, he was at the same time queerly enslaved by it. He could not seem to begin dismantling things, and invented every kind of excuse to postpone action. When I pointed this out to him he appeared unaccountably frightened. His father's old butler—who was there with other reacquired family servants—told me one day that Edward's occasional prowlings about the house, and especially down cellar, looked odd and unwholesome to him. I wondered if Asenath had been writing disturbing letters, but the butler said there was no mail which could have come from her.

VI.

It was about Christmas that Derby broke down one evening while calling on me. I was steering the conversation toward next summer's travels when he suddenly shrieked and leaped up from his chair with a look of shocking, uncontrollable fright—a cosmic panic and loathing such as only the nether gulfs of nightmare could bring to any sane mind.

"My brain! My brain! God, Dan—it's tugging—from beyond—knocking—clawing—that she-devil—even now—Ephraim—Kamog! Kamog!—The pit of the shoggoths—Iä! Shub-Niggurath! The Goat with a Thousand Young! ...

"The flame—the flame ... beyond body, beyond life ... in the earth ... oh, God! ..."

I pulled him back to his chair and poured some wine down his throat as his frenzy sank to a dull apathy. He did not resist, but kept his lips moving as if talking to himself. Presently I realised that he was trying to talk to me, and bent my ear to his mouth to catch the feeble words.

"... again, again ... she's trying ... I might have known ... nothing can stop that force; not distance, nor magic, nor death ... it comes and comes, mostly in the night ... I can't leave ... it's horrible ... oh, God, Dan, *if you only knew as I do just how horrible it is ....*"

When he had slumped down into a stupor I propped him with pillows and let normal sleep overtake him. I did not call a doctor, for I knew what would be said of his sanity, and wished to give nature a chance if I possibly could. He waked at midnight, and I put him to bed upstairs, but he was gone by morning. He had let himself quietly out of the house—and his butler, when called on the wire, said he was at home pacing restlessly about the library.

Edward went to pieces rapidly after that. He did not call again, but I went daily to see him. He would always be sitting in his library, staring at nothing and having an air of abnormal *listening*. Sometimes he talked rationally, but always on trivial topics. Any mention of his trouble, of future plans, or of Asenath would send him into a frenzy. His butler said he had frightful seizures at night, during which he might eventually do himself harm.

I had a long talk with his doctor, banker, and lawyer, and finally took the physician with two specialist colleagues to visit him. The spasms that resulted from the first questions were violent and pitiable—and that evening a closed car took his poor struggling body to the Arkham Sanitarium. I was made his guardian and called on him twice weekly—almost weeping to hear his wild shrieks, awesome whispers, and dreadful, droning repetitions of such phrases as "I had to do it—I had to do it ... it'll get me ... it'll get me ... down there ... down there in the dark. ... Mother, mother! Dan! Save me ... save me. ..."

How much hope of recovery there was, no one could say; but I tried my best to be optimistic. Edward must have a home if he emerged, so I transferred his servants to the Derby mansion, which would surely be his sane choice. What to do about the Crowninshield place with its complex arrangements and collections of utterly inexplicable objects I could not decide, so left it momentarily untouched—telling the Derby housemaid to go over and dust the chief rooms once a week, and ordering the furnace man to have a fire on those days.

The final nightmare came before Candlemas—heralded, in cruel irony, by a false gleam of hope. One morning late in January the sanitarium telephoned to report that Edward's reason had suddenly come back. His continuous memory, they said, was badly impaired; but sanity itself was certain. Of course he must remain some time for observation, but there could be little doubt of the outcome. All going well, he would surely be free in a week.

I hastened over in a flood of delight, but stood bewildered when a nurse took me to Edward's room. The patient rose to greet me, extending his hand with a polite smile; but I saw in an instant that he bore the strangely energised personality which had seemed so foreign to his own nature—the competent personality I had found so vaguely horrible, and which Edward himself had once vowed was the intruding soul of his wife. There was the same blazing vision—so like Asenath's and old Ephraim's—and the same firm mouth; and when he spoke I could sense the same grim, pervasive irony in his voice—the deep irony so redolent of potential evil. This was the person who had driven my car through the night five months before—the person I had not seen since that brief call when he had forgotten the old-time doorbell signal and stirred such nebulous fears in me—and now he filled me with the same dim feeling of blasphemous alienage and ineffable cosmic hideousness.

He spoke affably of arrangements for release—and there was nothing for me to do but assent, despite some remarkable gaps in his recent memories. Yet I felt that something was terribly, inexplicably wrong and abnormal. There were horrors in this thing that I could not reach. This was a sane person—but was it indeed the Edward Derby I had known? If not, who or what was it—*and where was Edward?* Ought it to be free or confined ... or ought it to be extirpated from the face of the earth? There was a hint of the abysmally sardonic in everything the creature said—the Asenath-like eyes lent a special and baffling mockery to certain words about the 'early liberty earned by an *especially close confinement.*' I must have behaved very awkwardly, and was glad to beat a retreat.

All that day and the next I racked my brain over the problem. What had happened? What sort of mind looked out through those alien eyes in Edward's face? I could think of nothing but this dimly terrible enigma, and gave up all efforts to perform my usual work. The second morning the hospital called up to say that the recovered patient was unchanged, and by evening I was close to a nervous collapse—a state I admit, though others will vow it coloured my subsequent vision. I have nothing to say on this point except that no madness of mine could account for all the evidence.

VII.

It was in the night—after that second evening—that stark, utter horror burst over me and weighted my spirit with a black, clutching panic from which it can never shake free. It began with a telephone call just before midnight. I was the only one up, and sleepily took down the receiver in the library. No one seemed to be on the wire, and I was about to hang up and go to bed when my ear caught a very faint suspicion of sound at the other end. Was someone trying under great difficulties to talk? As I listened I thought I heard a sort of half-liquid bubbling noise—"*glub ... glub ... glub*"—which had an odd suggestion of inarticulate, unintelligible word and syllable divisions. I called, "Who is it?" But the only answer was "*glub-glub ... glub-glub.*" I could only assume that the noise was mechanical; but fancying that it might be a case of a broken instrument able to receive but not to send, I added, "I can't hear you. Better hang up and try Information." Immediately I heard the receiver go on the hook at the other end.

This, I say, was just before midnight. When that call was traced afterward it was found to come from the old Crowninshield house, though it was fully half a week from the housemaid's day to be there. I shall only hint what was found at that house—the upheaval in a remote cellar storeroom, the tracks, the dirt, the hastily rifled wardrobe, the baffling marks on the telephone, the clumsily used stationery, and the detestable stench lingering over everything. The police, poor fools, have their smug little theories, and are still searching for those sinister discharged servants—who have dropped out of sight amidst the present furore. They speak of a ghoulish revenge for things that were done, and say I was included because I was Edward's best friend and adviser.

Idiots!—do they fancy those brutish clowns could have forged that handwriting? Do they fancy they could have brought what later came? Are they blind to the changes in that body that was Edward's? As for me, *I now believe all that Edward Derby ever told me.* There are horrors beyond life's edge that we do not suspect, and once in a while man's evil prying calls them just within our range. Ephraim—Asenath—that devil called them in, and they engulfed Edward as they are engulfing me.

Can I be sure that I am safe? Those powers survive the life of the physical form. The next day—in the afternoon, when I pulled out of my prostration and was able to walk and talk coherently—I went to the madhouse and shot him dead for Edward's and the world's sake, but can I be sure till he is cremated? They are keeping the body for some silly autopsies by different doctors—but I say he must be cremated. *He must be cremated—he who was not Edward Derby when I shot him.* I shall go mad if he is not, for I may be the next. But my will is not weak—and I shall not let it be undermined by the terrors I know are seething around it. One life—Ephraim, Asenath, and Edward—who now? I *will not* be driven out of my body ... I *will not* change souls with that bullet-ridden lich in the madhouse!

But let me try to tell coherently of that final horror. I will not speak of what the police persistently ignored—the tales of that dwarfed, grotesque, malodorous thing met by at least three wayfarers in High St. just before two o'clock, and the nature of the single footprints in certain places. I will say only that just about two the doorbell and knocker waked me—doorbell and knocker both, plied alternately and uncertainly in a kind of weak desperation, *and each trying to keep to Edward's old signal of three-and-two strokes.*

Roused from sound sleep, my mind leaped into a turmoil. Derby at the door—and remembering the old code! That new personality had not remembered it ... was Edward suddenly back in his rightful state? Why was he here in such evident stress and haste? Had he been released ahead of time, or had he escaped? Perhaps, I thought as I flung on a robe and bounded downstairs, his return to his own self had brought raving and violence, revoking his discharge and driving him to a desperate dash for freedom. Whatever had happened, he was good old Edward again, and I would help him!

When I opened the door into the elm-arched blackness a gust of insufferably foetid wind almost flung me prostrate. I choked in nausea, and for a second scarcely saw the dwarfed, humped figure on the steps. The summons had been Edward's, but who was this foul, stunted parody? Where had Edward had time to go? His ring had sounded only a second before the door opened.

The caller had on one of Edward's overcoats—its bottom almost touching the ground, and its sleeves rolled back yet still covering the hands. On the head was a slouch hat pulled low, while a black silk muffler concealed the face. As I stepped unsteadily forward, the figure made a semi-liquid sound like that I had heard over the telephone—"*glub … glub …*"—and thrust at me a large, closely written paper impaled on the end of a long pencil. Still reeling from the morbid and unaccountable foetor, I seized this paper and tried to read it in the light from the doorway.

Beyond question, it was in Edward's script. But why had he written when he was close enough to ring—and why was the script so awkward, coarse, and shaky? I could make out nothing in the dim half light, so edged back into the hall, the dwarf figure clumping mechanically after but pausing on the inner door's threshold. The odour of this singular messenger was really appalling, and I hoped (not in vain, thank God!) that my wife would not wake and confront it.

Then, as I read the paper, I felt my knees give under me and my vision go black. I was lying on the floor when I came to, that accursed sheet still clutched in my fear-rigid hand. This is what it said.

> *Dan—go to the sanitarium and kill it. Exterminate it. It isn't Edward Derby any more. She got me—it's Asenath—and she has been dead three months and a half. I lied when I said she had gone away. I killed her. I had to. It was sudden, but we were alone and I was in my right body. I saw a candlestick and smashed her head in. She would have got me for good at Hallowmass.*
>
> *"I buried her in the farther cellar storeroom under some old boxes and cleaned up all the traces. The servants suspected next morning, but they have such secrets that they dare not tell the police. I sent them off, but God knows what they—and others of the cult—will do.*

I thought for a while I was all right, and then I felt the tugging at my brain. I knew what it was—I ought to have remembered. A soul like hers—or Ephraim's—is half detached, and keeps right on after death as long as the body lasts. She was getting me—making me change bodies with her—seizing my body and putting me in that corpse of hers buried in the cellar.

I knew what was coming—that's why I snapped and had to go to the asylum. Then it came—I found myself choked in the dark—in Asenath's rotting carcass down there in the cellar under the boxes where I put it. And I knew she must be in my body at the sanitarium—permanently, for it was after Hallowmass, and the sacrifice would work even without her being there—sane, and ready for release as a menace to the world. I was desperate, and in spite of everything I clawed my way out.

I'm too far gone to talk—I couldn't manage to telephone—but I can still write. I'll get fixed up somehow and bring you this last word and warning. Kill that fiend *if you value the peace and comfort of the world.* See that it is cremated. *If you don't, it will live on and on, body to body forever, and I can't tell you what it will do. Keep clear of black magic, Dan, it's the devil's business. Goodbye—you've been a great friend. Tell the police whatever they'll believe—and I'm damnably sorry to drag all this on you. I'll be at peace before long—this thing won't hold together much more. Hope you can read this. And kill that thing—kill it.*

Yours—Ed.

It was only afterward that I read the last half of this paper, for I had fainted at the end of the third paragraph. I fainted again when I saw and smelled what cluttered up the threshold where the warm air had struck it. The messenger would not move or have consciousness any more.

The butler, tougher-fibred than I, did not faint at what met him in the hall in the morning. Instead, he telephoned the police. When they came I had been taken upstairs to bed, but the—other mass—lay where it had collapsed in the night. The men put handkerchiefs to their noses.

What they finally found inside Edward's oddly assorted clothes was mostly liquescent horror. There were bones, too—and a crushed-in skull. Some dental work positively identified the skull as Asenath's.

The Shunned House

I.

From even the greatest of horrors irony is seldom absent. Sometimes it enters directly into the composition of the events, while sometimes it relates only to their fortuitous position among persons and places. The latter sort is splendidly exemplified by a case in the ancient city of Providence, where in the late forties Edgar Allan Poe used to sojourn often during his unsuccessful wooing of the gifted poetess, Mrs. Whitman. Poe generally stopped at the Mansion House in Benefit Street—the renamed Golden Ball Inn whose roof has sheltered Washington, Jefferson, and Lafayette—and his favourite walk led northward along the same street to Mrs. Whitman's home and the neighbouring hillside churchyard of St. John's, whose hidden expanse of eighteenth-century gravestones had for him a peculiar fascination.

Now the irony is this. In this walk, so many times repeated, the world's greatest master of the terrible and the bizarre was obliged to pass a particular house on the eastern side of the street; a dingy, antiquated structure perched on the abruptly rising side-hill, with a great unkempt yard dating from a time when the region was partly open country. It does not appear that he ever wrote or spoke of it, nor is there any evidence that he even noticed it. And yet that house, to the two persons in possession of certain information, equals or outranks in horror the wildest phantasy of the genius who so often passed it unknowingly, and stands starkly leering as a symbol of all that is unutterably hideous.

The house was—and for that matter still is—of a kind to attract the attention of the curious. Originally a farm or semi-farm building, it followed the average New England colonial lines of the middle eighteenth century—the prosperous peaked-roof sort, with two stories and dormerless attic, and with the Georgian doorway and interior panelling dictated by the progress of taste at that time. It faced south, with one gable end buried to the lower windows in the eastward rising hill, and the other exposed to the foundations toward the street. Its construction, over a century and a half ago, had followed the grading and straightening of the road in that especial vicinity; for Benefit Street—at first called Back Street—was laid out as a lane winding amongst the graveyards of the first settlers, and straightened only when the removal of the bodies to the North Burial Ground made it decently possible to cut through the old family plots.

At the start, the western wall had lain some twenty feet up a precipitous lawn from the roadway; but a widening of the street at about the time of the Revolution sheared off most of the intervening space, exposing the foundations so that a brick basement wall had to be made, giving the deep cellar a street frontage with door and two windows above ground, close to the new line of public travel. When the sidewalk was laid out a century ago the last of the intervening space was removed; and Poe in his walks must have seen only a sheer ascent of dull grey brick flush with the sidewalk and surmounted at a height of ten feet by the antique shingled bulk of the house proper.

The farm-like grounds extended back very deeply up the hill, almost to Wheaton Street. The space south of the house, abutting on Benefit Street, was of course greatly above the existing sidewalk level, forming a terrace bounded by a high bank wall of damp, mossy stone pierced by a steep flight of narrow steps which led inward between canyon-like surfaces to the upper region of mangy lawn, rheumy brick walls, and neglected gardens whose dismantled cement urns, rusted kettles fallen from tripods of knotty sticks, and similar paraphernalia set off the weather-beaten front door with its broken fanlight, rotting Ionic pilasters, and wormy triangular pediment.

What I heard in my youth about the shunned house was merely that people died there in alarmingly great numbers. That, I was told, was why the original owners had moved out some twenty years after building the place. It was plainly unhealthy, perhaps because of the dampness and fungous growth in the cellar, the general sickish smell, the draughts of the hallways, or the quality of the well and pump water. These things were bad enough, and these were all that gained belief among the persons whom I knew. Only the notebooks of my antiquarian uncle, Dr. Elihu Whipple, revealed to me at length the darker, vaguer surmises which formed an undercurrent of folklore among old-time servants and humble folk; surmises which never travelled far, and which were largely forgotten when Providence grew to be a metropolis with a shifting modern population.

The general fact is, that the house was never regarded by the solid part of the community as in any real sense "haunted." There were no widespread tales of rattling chains, cold currents of air, extinguished lights, or faces at the window. Extremists sometimes said the house was "unlucky", but that is as far as even they went. What was really beyond dispute is that a frightful proportion of persons died there; or more accurately, had died there, since after some peculiar happenings over sixty years ago the building had become deserted through the sheer impossibility of renting it. These persons were not all cut off suddenly by any one cause; rather did it seem that their vitality was insidiously sapped, so that each one died the sooner from whatever tendency to weakness he may have naturally had. And those who did not die displayed in varying degree a type of anaemia or consumption, and sometimes a decline of the mental faculties, which spoke ill for the salubriousness of the building. Neighbouring houses, it must be added, seemed entirely free from the noxious quality.

This much I knew before my insistent questioning led my uncle to shew me the notes which finally embarked us both on our hideous investigation. In my childhood the shunned house was vacant, with barren, gnarled, and terrible old trees, long, queerly pale grass, and nightmarishly misshapen weeds in the high terraced yard where birds never lingered. We boys used to overrun the place, and I can still recall my youthful terror not only at the morbid strangeness of this sinister vegetation, but at the eldritch atmosphere and odour of the dilapidated house, whose unlocked front door was often entered in quest of shudders. The small-paned windows were largely broken, and a nameless air of desolation hung round the precarious panelling, shaky interior shutters, peeling wall-paper, falling plaster, rickety staircases, and such fragments of battered furniture as still remained. The dust and cobwebs added their touch of the fearful; and brave indeed was the boy who would voluntarily ascend the ladder to the attic, a vast raftered length lighted only by small blinking windows in the gable ends, and filled with a massed wreckage of chests, chairs, and spinning-wheels which infinite years of deposit had shrouded and festooned into monstrous and hellish shapes.

But after all, the attic was not the most terrible part of the house. It was the dank, humid cellar which somehow exerted the strongest repulsion on us, even though it was wholly above ground on the street side, with only a thin door and window-pierced brick wall to separate it from the busy sidewalk. We scarcely knew whether to haunt it in spectral fascination, or to shun it for the sake of our souls and our sanity. For one thing, the bad odour of the house was strongest there; and for another thing, we did not like the white fungous growths which occasionally sprang up in rainy summer weather from the hard earth floor. Those fungi, grotesquely like the vegetation in the yard outside, were truly horrible in their outlines; detestable parodies of toadstools and Indian pipes, whose like we had never seen in any other situation. They rotted quickly, and at one stage became slightly phosphorescent; so that nocturnal passers-by sometimes spoke of witch-fires glowing behind the broken panes of the foetor-spreading windows.

We never—even in our wildest Hallowe'en moods—visited this cellar by night, but in some of our daytime visits could detect the phos-phorescence, especially when the day was dark and wet. There was also a subtler thing we often thought we detected—a very strange thing which was, however, merely suggestive at most. I refer to a sort of cloudy whitish pattern on the dirt floor—a vague, shifting deposit of mould or nitre which we sometimes thought we could trace amidst the sparse fungous growths near the huge fireplace of the basement kitchen. Once in a while it struck us that this patch bore an uncanny resemblance to a doubled-up human figure, though generally no such kinship existed, and often there was no whitish deposit whatever. On a certain rainy afternoon when this illusion seemed phenomenally strong, and when, in addition, I had fancied I glimpsed a kind of thin, yellowish, shimmering exhalation rising from the nitrous pattern toward the yawning fireplace, I spoke to my uncle about the matter. He smiled at this odd conceit, but it seemed that his smile was tinged with reminiscence. Later I heard that a similar notion entered into some of the wild ancient tales of the common folk—a notion likewise alluding to ghoulish, wolfish shapes taken by smoke from the great chimney, and queer contours assumed by certain of the sinuous tree-roots that thrust their way into the cellar through the loose foundation-stones.

II.

Not till my adult years did my uncle set before me the notes and data which he had collected concerning the shunned house. Dr. Whipple was a sane, conservative physician of the old school, and for all his interest in the place was not eager to encourage young thoughts toward the abnormal. His own view, postulating simply a building and location of markedly unsanitary qualities, had nothing to do with abnormality; but he realised that the very picturesqueness which aroused his own interest would in a boy's fanciful mind take on all manner of gruesome imaginative associations.

The doctor was a bachelor; a white-haired, clean-shaven, old-fashioned gentleman, and a local historian of note, who had often broken a lance with such controversial guardians of tradition as

Sidney S. Rider and Thomas W. Bicknell. He lived with one manservant in a Georgian homestead with knocker and iron-railed steps, balanced eerily on a steep ascent of North Court Street beside the ancient brick court and colony house where his grandfather—a cousin of that celebrated privateersman, Capt. Whipple, who burnt His Majesty's armed schooner *Gaspee* in 1772—had voted in the legislature on May 4, 1776, for the independence of the Rhode Island Colony. Around him in the damp, low-ceiled library with the musty white panelling, heavy carved overmantel, and small-paned, vine-shaded windows, were the relics and records of his ancient family, among which were many dubious allusions to the shunned house in Benefit Street. That pest spot lies not far distant—for Benefit runs ledgewise just above the court-house along the precipitous hill up which the first settlement climbed.

When, in the end, my insistent pestering and maturing years evoked from my uncle the hoarded lore I sought, there lay before me a strange enough chronicle. Long-winded, statistical, and drearily genealogical as some of the matter was, there ran through it a continuous thread of brooding, tenacious horror and preternatural malevolence which impressed me even more than it had impressed the good doctor. Separate events fitted together uncannily, and seemingly irrelevant details held mines of hideous possibilities. A new and burning curiosity grew in me, compared to which my boyish curiosity was feeble and inchoate. The first revelation led to an exhaustive research, and finally to that shuddering quest which proved so disastrous to myself and mine. For at last my uncle insisted on joining the search I had commenced, and after a certain night in that house he did not come away with me. I am lonely without that gentle soul whose long years were filled only with honour, virtue, good taste, benevolence, and learning. I have reared a marble urn to his memory in St. John's churchyard—the place that Poe loved—the hidden grove of giant willows on the hill, where tombs and headstones huddle quietly between the hoary bulk of the church and the houses and bank walls of Benefit Street.

The history of the house, opening amidst a maze of dates, revealed no trace of the sinister either about its construction or about the prosperous and honourable family who built it. Yet from the first a taint of calamity, soon increased to boding significance, was apparent. My uncle's carefully compiled record began with the building of the structure in 1763, and followed the theme with an unusual amount of detail. The shunned house, it seems, was first inhabited by William

Harris and his wife Rhoby Dexter, with their children, Elkanah, born in 1755, Abigail, born in 1757, William, Jr., born in 1759, and Ruth, born in 1761. Harris was a substantial merchant and seaman in the West India trade, connected with the firm of Obadiah Brown and his nephews. After Brown's death in 1761, the new firm of Nicholas Brown & Co. made him master of the brig *Prudence*, Providence-built, of 120 tons, thus enabling him to erect the new homestead he had desired ever since his marriage.

The site he had chosen—a recently straightened part of the new and fashionable Back Street, which ran along the side of the hill above crowded Cheapside—was all that could be wished, and the building did justice to the location. It was the best that moderate means could afford, and Harris hastened to move in before the birth of a fifth child which the family expected. That child, a boy, came in December; but was still-born. Nor was any child to be born alive in that house for a century and a half.

The next April sickness occurred among the children, and Abigail and Ruth died before the month was over. Dr. Job Ives diagnosed the trouble as some infantile fever, though others declared it was more of a mere wasting-away or decline. It seemed, in any event, to be contagious; for Hannah Bowen, one of the two servants, died of it in the following June. Eli Liddeason, the other servant, constantly complained of weakness; and would have returned to his father's farm in Rehoboth but for a sudden attachment for Mehitabel Pierce, who was hired to succeed Hannah. He died the next year—a sad year indeed, since it marked the death of William Harris himself, enfeebled as he was by the climate of Martinique, where his occupation had kept him for considerable periods during the preceding decade.

The widowed Rhoby Harris never recovered from the shock of her husband's death, and the passing of her first-born Elkanah two years later was the final blow to her reason. In 1768 she fell victim to a mild form of insanity, and was thereafter confined to the upper part of the house; her elder maiden sister, Mercy Dexter, having moved in to take charge of the family. Mercy was a plain, raw-boned woman of great strength; but her health visibly declined from the time of her advent. She was greatly devoted to her unfortunate sister, and had an especial affection for her only surviving nephew William, who from a sturdy infant had become a sickly, spindling lad. In this year the servant Mehitabel died, and the other servant, Preserved Smith, left without coherent explanation—or at least, with only some wild tales and a complaint that he disliked the smell of the place. For a time Mercy could secure no more help, since the seven deaths and case of madness, all occurring within five years' space, had begun to set in motion the body of fireside rumour which later became so bizarre. Ultimately, however, she obtained new servants from out of town; Ann White, a morose woman from that part of North Kingstown now set off as the township of Exeter, and a capable Boston man named Zenas Low.

It was Ann White who first gave definite shape to the sinister idle talk. Mercy should have known better than to hire anyone from the Nooseneck Hill country, for that remote bit of backwoods was then, as now, a seat of the most uncomfortable superstitions. As lately as 1892 an Exeter community exhumed a dead body and ceremoniously burnt its heart in order to prevent certain alleged visitations injurious to the public health and peace, and one may imagine the point of view of the same section in 1768. Ann's tongue was perniciously active, and within a few months Mercy discharged her, filling her place with a faithful and amiable Amazon from Newport, Maria Robbins.

Meanwhile poor Rhoby Harris, in her madness, gave voice to dreams and imaginings of the most hideous sort. At times her screams became insupportable, and for long periods she would utter shrieking horrors which necessitated her son's temporary residence with his cousin, Peleg Harris, in Presbyterian-Lane near the new college building. The boy would seem to improve after these visits, and had Mercy been as wise as she was well-meaning, she would have let him live permanently with Peleg. Just what Mrs. Harris cried out in her fits of violence, tradition hesitates to say; or rather, presents such extravagant accounts that they nullify themselves through sheer absurdity. Certainly it sounds absurd to hear that a woman educated only in the rudiments of French often shouted for hours in a coarse and idiomatic form of that language, or that the same person, alone and guarded, complained wildly of a staring thing which bit and chewed at her. In 1772 the servant Zenas died, and when Mrs. Harris heard of it she laughed with a shocking delight utterly foreign to her. The next year she herself died, and was laid to rest in the North Burial Ground beside her husband.

Upon the outbreak of trouble with Great Britain in 1775, William Harris, despite his scant sixteen years and feeble constitution, managed to enlist in the Army of Observation under General Greene; and from that time on enjoyed a steady rise in health and prestige. In 1780, as a Captain in Rhode Island forces in New Jersey under Colonel Angell, he met and married Phebe Hetfield of Elizabethtown, whom he brought to Providence upon his honourable discharge in the following year.

The young soldier's return was not a thing of unmitigated happiness. The house, it is true, was still in good condition; and the street had been widened and changed in name from Back Street to Benefit Street. But Mercy Dexter's once robust frame had undergone a sad and curious decay, so that she was now a stooped and pathetic figure with hollow voice and disconcerting pallor—qualities shared to a singular degree by the one remaining servant Maria. In the autumn of 1782 Phebe Harris gave birth to a still-born daughter, and on the fifteenth of the next May Mercy Dexter took leave of a useful, austere, and virtuous life.

William Harris, at last thoroughly convinced of the radically unhealthful nature of his abode, now took steps toward quitting it and closing it forever. Securing temporary quarters for himself and his wife at the newly opened Golden Ball Inn, he arranged for the building of a new and finer house in Westminster Street, in the growing part of the town across the Great Bridge. There, in 1785, his son Dutee was born; and there the family dwelt till the encroachments of commerce drove them back across the river and over the hill to Angell Street, in the newer East Side residence district, where the late Archer Harris built his sumptuous but hideous French-roofed mansion in 1876. William and Phebe both succumbed to the yellow fever epidemic of 1797, but Dutee was brought up by his cousin Rathbone Harris, Peleg's son.

Rathbone was a practical man, and rented the Benefit Street house despite William's wish to keep it vacant. He considered it an obligation to his ward to make the most of all the boy's property, nor did he concern himself with the deaths and illnesses which caused so many changes of tenants, or the steadily growing aversion with which the house was generally regarded. It is likely that he felt only vexation when, in 1804, the town council ordered him to fumigate the place with sulphur, tar, and gum camphor on account of the much-discussed deaths of four persons, presumably caused by the then diminishing fever epidemic. They said the place had a febrile smell.

Dutee himself thought little of the house, for he grew up to be a privateersman, and served with distinction on the *Vigilant* under Capt. Cahoone in the War of 1812. He returned unharmed, married in 1814, and became a father on that memorable night of September 23, 1815, when a great gale drove the waters of the bay over half the town, and floated a tall sloop well up Westminster Street so that its masts almost tapped the Harris windows in symbolic affirmation that the new boy, Welcome, was a seaman's son.

Welcome did not survive his father, but lived to perish gloriously at Fredericksburg in 1862. Neither he nor his son Archer knew of the shunned house as other than a nuisance almost impossible to rent—perhaps on account of the mustiness and sickly odour of unkempt old age. Indeed, it never was rented after a series of deaths culminating in 1861, which the excitement of the war tended to throw into obscurity. Carrington Harris, last of the male line, knew it only as a deserted and somewhat picturesque centre of legend until I told him my experience. He had meant to tear it down and build an apartment house on the site, but after my account decided to let it stand, install plumbing, and rent it. Nor has he yet had any difficulty in obtaining tenants. The horror has gone.

III.

It may well be imagined how powerfully I was affected by the annals of the Harrises. In this continuous record there seemed to me to brood a persistent evil beyond anything in Nature as I had known it; an evil clearly connected with the house and not with the family. This impression was confirmed by my uncle's less systematic array of miscellaneous data—legends transcribed from servant gossip, cuttings from the papers, copies of death-certificates by fellow-physicians, and the like. All of this material I cannot hope to give, for my uncle was a tireless antiquarian and very deeply interested in the shunned house; but I may refer to several dominant points which earn notice by their recurrence through many reports from diverse sources. For example, the servant gossip was practically unanimous in attributing to the fungous and malodorous cellar of the house a vast supremacy in evil influence. There had been servants—Ann White especially—who would not use the cellar kitchen, and at least three well-defined legends bore upon the queer quasi-human or diabolic outlines assumed by tree-roots and patches of mould in that region. These latter narratives interested me profoundly, on account of what I had seen in my boyhood, but I felt that most of the significance had in each case been largely obscured by additions from the common stock of local ghost lore.

Ann White, with her Exeter superstition, had promulgated the most extravagant and at the same time most consistent tale; alleging that there must lie buried beneath the house one of those vampires—

the dead who retain their bodily form and live on the blood or breath of the living—whose hideous legions send their preying shapes or spirits abroad by night. To destroy a vampire one must, the grandmothers say, exhume it and burn its heart, or at least drive a stake through that organ; and Ann's dogged insistence on a search under the cellar had been prominent in bringing about her discharge.

Her tales, however, commanded a wide audience, and were the more readily accepted because the house indeed stood on land once used for burial purposes. To me their interest depended less on this circumstance than on the peculiarly appropriate way in which they dovetailed with certain other things—the complaint of the departing servant Preserved Smith, who had preceded Ann and never heard of her, that something "sucked his breath" at night; the death-certificates of fever victims of 1804, issued by Dr. Chad Hopkins, and shewing the four deceased persons all unaccountably lacking in blood; and the obscure passages of poor Rhoby Harris's ravings, where she complained of the sharp teeth of a glassy-eyed, half-visible presence.

Free from unwarranted superstition though I am, these things produced in me an odd sensation, which was intensified by a pair of widely separated newspaper cuttings relating to deaths in the shunned house—one from the Providence Gazette and Country-Journal of April 12, 1815, and the other from the Daily Transcript and Chronicle of October 27, 1845—each of which detailed an appallingly grisly circumstance whose duplication was remarkable. It seems that in both instances the dying person, in 1815 a gentle old lady named Stafford and in 1845 a school-teacher of middle age named Eleazar Durfee, became transfigured in a horrible way; glaring glassily and attempting to bite the throat of the attending physician. Even more puzzling, though, was the final case which put an end to the renting of the house—a series of anaemia deaths preceded by progressive madnesses wherein the patient would craftily attempt the lives of his relatives by incisions in the neck or wrist.

This was in 1860 and 1861, when my uncle had just begun his medical practice; and before leaving for the front he heard much of it from his elder professional colleagues. The really inexplicable thing was the way in which the victims—ignorant people, for the ill-smelling and widely shunned house could now be rented to no others—would babble maledictions in French, a language they could not possibly have studied to any extent. It made one think of poor Rhoby Harris nearly a century before, and so moved my uncle that he commenced collecting historical data on the house after listening, some time subsequent to his return from the war, to the first-hand account of Drs. Chase and Whitmarsh. Indeed, I could see that my uncle had thought deeply on the subject, and that he was glad of my own interest—an open-minded and sympathetic interest which enabled him to discuss with me matters at which others would merely have laughed. His fancy had not gone so far as mine, but he felt that the place was rare in its imaginative potentialities, and worthy of note as an inspiration in the field of the grotesque and macabre.

For my part, I was disposed to take the whole subject with profound seriousness, and began at once not only to review the evidence, but to accumulate as much more as I could. I talked with the elderly Archer Harris, then owner of the house, many times before his death in 1916; and obtained from him and his still surviving maiden sister Alice an authentic corroboration of all the family data my uncle had collected. When, however, I asked them what connexion with France or its language the house could have, they confessed themselves as frankly baffled and ignorant as I. Archer knew nothing, and all that Miss Harris could say was that an old allusion her grandfather, Dutee Harris, had heard of might have shed a little light. The old seaman, who had survived his son Welcome's death in battle by two years, had not himself known the legend; but recalled that his earliest nurse, the ancient Maria Robbins, seemed darkly aware of something that might have lent a weird significance to the French ravings of Rhoby Harris, which she had so often heard during the last days of that hapless woman. Maria had been at the shunned house from 1769 till the removal of the family in 1783, and had seen Mercy Dexter die. Once she hinted to the child Dutee of a somewhat peculiar circumstance in Mercy's last moments, but he had soon forgotten all about it save that it was something peculiar. The granddaughter, moreover, recalled even this much with difficulty. She and her brother were not so much interested in the house as was Archer's son Carrington, the present owner, with whom I talked after my experience.

Having exhausted the Harris family of all the information it could furnish, I turned my attention to early town records and deeds with a zeal more penetrating than that which my uncle had occasionally shewn in the same work. What I wished was a comprehensive history of the site from its very settlement in 1636—or even before, if any Narragansett Indian legend could be unearthed to supply the data. I found, at the start, that the land had been part of the long strip of home lot granted originally to John Throckmorton; one of many similar strips beginning at the Town Street beside the river and extending up over the hill to a line roughly corresponding with the modern Hope Street. The Throckmorton lot had later, of course, been much subdivided; and I became very assiduous in tracing that section through which Back or Benefit Street was later run. It had, a rumour indeed said, been the Throckmorton graveyard; but as I examined the records more carefully, I found that the graves had all been transferred at an early date to the North Burial Ground on the Pawtucket West Road.

Then suddenly I came—by a rare piece of chance, since it was not in the main body of records and might easily have been missed—upon something which aroused my keenest eagerness, fitting in as it did with several of the queerest phases of the affair. It was the record of a lease, in 1697, of a small tract of ground to an Etienne Roulet and wife. At last the French element had appeared—that, and another deeper element of horror which the name conjured up from the darkest recesses of my weird and heterogeneous reading—and I feverishly studied the platting of the locality as it had been before the cutting through and partial straightening of Back Street between 1747 and 1758. I found what I had half expected, that where the shunned house now stood the Roulets had laid out their graveyard behind a one-story and attic cottage, and that no record of any transfer of graves existed. The document, indeed, ended in much confusion; and I was forced to ransack both the Rhode Island Historical Society and Shepley Library before I could find a local door which the name Etienne Roulet would unlock. In the end I did find something; something of such vague but monstrous import that I set about at once to examine the cellar of the shunned house itself with a new and excited minuteness.

The Roulets, it seemed, had come in 1696 from East Greenwich, down the west shore of Narragansett Bay. They were Huguenots from Caude, and had encountered much opposition before the Providence selectmen allowed them to settle in the town. Unpopularity had dogged them in East Greenwich, whither they had come in 1686, after the revocation of the Edict of Nantes, and rumour said that the cause of dislike extended beyond mere racial and national prejudice, or the land disputes which involved other French settlers with the English in rivalries which not even Governor Andros could quell. But their ardent Protestantism—too ardent, some whispered—and their evident distress when virtually driven from the village down the bay, had moved the sympathy of the town fathers. Here the strangers had been granted a haven; and the swarthy Etienne Roulet, less apt at agriculture than at reading queer books and drawing queer diagrams, was given a clerical post in the warehouse at Pardon Tillinghast's wharf, far south in Town Street. There had, however, been a riot of some sort later on—perhaps forty years later, after old Roulet's death—and no one seemed to hear of the family after that.

For a century and more, it appeared, the Roulets had been well remembered and frequently discussed as vivid incidents in the quiet life of a New England seaport. Etienne's son Paul, a surly fellow whose erratic conduct had probably provoked the riot which wiped out the family, was particularly a source of speculation; and though Providence never shared the witchcraft panics of her Puritan neighbours, it was freely intimated by old wives that his prayers were neither uttered at the proper time nor directed toward the proper object. All this had undoubtedly formed the basis of the legend known by old Maria Robbins. What relation it had to the French ravings of Rhoby Harris and other inhabitants of the shunned house, imagination or future discovery alone could determine. I wondered how many of those who had known the legends realised that additional link with the terrible which my wide reading had given me; that ominous item in the annals of morbid horror which tells of the creature *Jacques Roulet, of Caude*, who in 1598 was condemned to death as a daemoniac but afterward saved from the stake by the Paris parliament and shut in a madhouse. He had been found covered with blood and shreds of flesh in a wood, shortly after the killing and rending of a boy by a pair of wolves. One wolf was seen to lope away unhurt. Surely a pretty hearthside tale, with a queer significance as to name and place; but I decided that the Providence gossips could not have generally known of it. Had they known, the coincidence of names would have brought some drastic and frightened action— indeed, might not its limited whispering have precipitated the final riot which erased the Roulets from the town?

I now visited the accursed place with increased frequency; studying the unwholesome vegetation of the garden, examining all the walls of the building, and poring over every inch of the earthen cellar floor. Finally, with Carrington Harris's permission, I fitted a key to the disused door opening from the cellar directly upon Benefit Street, preferring to have a more immediate access to the outside world than the dark stairs, ground floor hall, and front door could give. There, where morbidity lurked most thickly, I searched and poked during long afternoons when the sunlight filtered in through the cobwebbed above-ground windows, and a sense of security glowed from the unlocked door which placed me only a few feet from the placid sidewalk outside. Nothing new rewarded my efforts—only the same depressing mustiness and faint suggestions of noxious odours and nitrous outlines on the floor—and I fancy that many pedestrians must have watched me curiously through the broken panes.

At length, upon a suggestion of my uncle's, I decided to try the spot nocturnally; and one stormy midnight ran the beams of an electric torch over the mouldy floor with its uncanny shapes and distorted, half-phosphorescent fungi. The place had dispirited me curiously that evening, and I was almost prepared when I saw—or thought I saw—amidst the whitish deposits a particularly sharp definition of the "huddled form" I had suspected from boyhood. Its clearness was astonishing and unprecedented—and as I watched I seemed to see again the thin, yellowish, shimmering exhalation which had startled me on that rainy afternoon so many years before.

Above the anthropomorphic patch of mould by the fireplace it rose; a subtle, sickish, almost luminous vapour which as it hung trembling in the dampness seemed to develop vague and shocking suggestions of form, gradually trailing off into nebulous decay and passing up into the blackness of the great chimney with a foetor in its wake. It was truly horrible, and the more so to me because of what I knew of the spot. Refusing to flee, I watched it fade—and as I watched I felt that it was in turn watching me greedily with eyes more imaginable than visible. When I told my uncle about it he was greatly aroused; and after a tense hour of reflection, arrived at a definite and drastic decision. Weighing in his mind the importance of the matter, and the significance of our relation to it, he insisted that we both test—and if possible destroy—the horror of the house by a joint night or nights of aggressive vigil in that musty and fungus-cursed cellar.

IV.

On Wednesday, June 25, 1919, after a proper notification of Carrington Harris which did not include surmises as to what we expected to find, my uncle and I conveyed to the shunned house two camp chairs and a folding camp cot, together with some scientific mechanism of greater weight and intricacy. These we placed in the cellar during the day, screening the windows with paper and planning to return in the evening for our first vigil. We had locked the door from the cellar to the ground floor; and having a key to the outside cellar door, we were prepared to leave our expensive and delicate apparatus—which we had obtained secretly and at great cost—as many days as our vigils might need to be protracted. It was our design to sit up together till very late, and then watch singly till dawn in two-hour stretches, myself first and then my companion; the inactive member resting on the cot.

The natural leadership with which my uncle procured the instruments from the laboratories of Brown University and the Cranston Street Armoury, and instinctively assumed direction of our venture, was a marvellous commentary on the potential vitality and resilience of a man of eighty-one. Elihu Whipple had lived according to the hygienic laws he had preached as a physician, and but for what happened later would be here in full vigour today. Only two persons suspect what did happen—Carrington Harris and myself. I had to tell Harris because he owned the house and deserved to know what had gone out of it. Then too, we had spoken to him in advance of our quest; and I felt after my uncle's going that he would understand and assist me in some vitally necessary public explanations. He turned very pale, but agreed to help me, and decided that it would now be safe to rent the house.

To declare that we were not nervous on that rainy night of watching would be an exaggeration both gross and ridiculous. We were not, as I have said, in any sense childishly superstitious, but scientific study and reflection had taught us that the known universe of three dimensions embraces the merest fraction of the whole cosmos of substance and energy. In this case an overwhelming preponderance of evidence from numerous authentic sources pointed to the tenacious existence of certain forces of great power and, so far as the human point of view is concerned, exceptional malignancy. To say that we actually believed in vampires or werewolves would be a carelessly inclusive statement. Rather must it be said that we were not prepared to deny the possibility of certain unfamiliar and unclassified modifications of vital force and attenuated matter; existing very infrequently in three-dimensional space because of its more intimate connexion with other spatial units, yet close enough to the boundary of our own to furnish us occasional manifestations which we, for lack of a proper vantage-point, may never hope to understand.

In short, it seemed to my uncle and me that an incontrovertible array of facts pointed to some lingering influence in the shunned house; traceable to one or another of the ill-favoured French settlers of two centuries before, and still operative through rare and unknown laws of atomic and electronic motion. That the family of Roulet had possessed an abnormal affinity for outer circles of entity—dark spheres which for normal folk hold only repulsion and terror—their recorded history seemed to prove. Had not, then, the riots of those bygone seventeen-thirties set moving certain kinetic patterns in the morbid brain of one or more of them—notably the sinister Paul Roulet—which obscurely survived the bodies murdered and buried by the mob, and continued to function in some multiple-dimensioned space along the original lines of force determined by a frantic hatred of the encroaching community?

Such a thing was surely not a physical or biochemical impossibility in the light of a newer science which includes the theories of relativity and intra-atomic action. One might easily imagine an alien nucleus of substance or energy, formless or otherwise, kept alive by imperceptible or immaterial subtractions from the life-force or bodily tissues and fluids of other and more palpably living things into which it penetrates and with whose fabric it sometimes completely merges itself. It might be actively hostile, or it might be dictated merely by blind motives of self-preservation. In any case such a monster must of necessity be in our scheme of things an anomaly and an intruder, whose extirpation forms a primary duty with every man not an enemy to the world's life, health, and sanity.

What baffled us was our utter ignorance of the aspect in which we might encounter the thing. No sane person had even seen it, and few had ever felt it definitely. It might be pure energy—a form ethereal and outside the realm of substance—or it might be partly material; some unknown and equivocal mass of plasticity, capable of changing at will to nebulous approximations of the solid, liquid, gaseous, or tenuously unparticled states. The anthropomorphic patch of mould on the floor, the form of the yellowish vapour, and the curvature of the tree-roots in some of the old tales, all argued at least a remote and reminiscent connexion with the human shape; but how representative or permanent that similarity might be, none could say with any kind of certainty.

We had devised two weapons to fight it; a large and specially fitted Crookes tube operated by powerful storage batteries and provided with peculiar screens and reflectors, in case it proved intangible and opposable only by vigorously destructive ether radiations, and a pair of military flame-throwers of the sort used in the world-war, in case it proved partly material and susceptible of mechanical destruction— for like the superstitious Exeter rustics, we were prepared to burn the thing's heart out if heart existed to burn. All this aggressive mechanism we set in the cellar in positions carefully arranged with reference to the cot and chairs, and to the spot before the fireplace where the mould had taken strange shapes. That suggestive patch, by the way, was only faintly visible when we placed our furniture and instruments, and when we returned that evening for the actual vigil. For a moment I half doubted that I had ever seen it in the more definitely limned form—but then I thought of the legends.

Our cellar vigil began at 10 p.m., daylight saving time, and as it continued we found no promise of pertinent developments. A weak, filtered glow from the rain-harassed street-lamps outside, and a feeble phosphorescence from the detestable fungi within, shewed the dripping stone of the walls, from which all traces of whitewash had vanished; the dank, foetid, and mildew-tainted hard earth floor with its obscene fungi; the rotting remains of what had been stools, chairs, and tables, and other more shapeless furniture; the heavy planks and massive beams of the ground floor overhead; the decrepit plank door leading to bins and chambers beneath other parts of the house; the crumbling stone staircase with ruined wooden hand-rail; and the crude and cavernous fireplace of blackened brick where rusted iron fragments revealed the past presence of hooks, andirons, spit, crane, and a door to the Dutch oven—these things, and our austere cot and camp chairs, and the heavy and intricate destructive machinery we had brought.

We had, as in my own former explorations, left the door to the street unlocked; so that a direct and practical path of escape might lie open in case of manifestations beyond our power to deal with. It was our idea that our continued nocturnal presence would call forth whatever malign entity lurked there; and that being prepared, we could dispose of the thing with one or the other of our provided means as soon as we had recognised and observed it sufficiently. How long it might require to evoke and extinguish the thing, we had no notion. It occurred to us, too, that our venture was far from safe; for in what strength the thing might appear no one could tell. But we deemed the game worth the hazard, and embarked on it alone and unhesitatingly; conscious that the seeking of outside aid would only expose us to ridicule and perhaps defeat our entire purpose. Such was our frame of mind as we talked—far into the night, till my uncle's growing drowsiness made me remind him to lie down for his two-hour sleep.

Something like fear chilled me as I sat there in the small hours alone—I say alone, for one who sits by a sleeper is indeed alone;

perhaps more alone than he can realise. My uncle breathed heavily, his deep inhalations and exhalations accompanied by the rain outside, and punctuated by another nerve-racking sound of distant dripping water within—for the house was repulsively damp even in dry weather, and in this storm positively swamp-like. I studied the loose, antique masonry of the walls in the fungus-light and the feeble rays which stole in from the street through the screened windows; and once, when the noisome atmosphere of the place seemed about to sicken me, I opened the door and looked up and down the street, feasting my eyes on familiar sights and my nostrils on the wholesome air. Still nothing occurred to reward my watching; and I yawned repeatedly, fatigue getting the better of apprehension.

Then the stirring of my uncle in his sleep attracted my notice. He had turned restlessly on the cot several times during the latter half of the first hour, but now he was breathing with unusual irregularity, occasionally heaving a sigh which held more than a few of the qualities of a choking moan. I turned my electric flashlight on him and found his face averted, so rising and crossing to the other side of the cot, I again flashed the light to see if he seemed in any pain. What I saw unnerved me most surprisingly, considering its relative triviality. It must have been merely the association of any odd circumstance with the sinister nature of our location and mission, for surely the circumstance was not in itself frightful or unnatural. It was merely that my uncle's facial expression, disturbed no doubt by the strange dreams which our situation prompted, betrayed considerable agitation, and seemed not at all characteristic of him. His habitual expression was one of kindly and well-bred calm, whereas now a variety of emotions seemed struggling within him. I think, on the whole, that it was this *variety* which chiefly disturbed me. My uncle, as he gasped and tossed in increasing perturbation and with eyes that had now started open, seemed not one but many men, and suggested a curious quality of alienage from himself.

All at once he commenced to mutter, and I did not like the look of his mouth and teeth as he spoke. The words were at first indistinguishable, and then—with a tremendous start—I recognised something about them which filled me with icy fear till I recalled the breadth of my uncle's education and the interminable translations he had made from anthropological and antiquarian articles in the *Revue des Deux Mondes.* For the venerable Elihu Whipple was muttering in *French,* and the few phrases I could distinguish seemed connected with the darkest myths he had ever adapted from the famous Paris magazine.

Suddenly a perspiration broke out on the sleeper's forehead, and he leaped abruptly up, half awake. The jumble of French changed to a cry in English, and the hoarse voice shouted excitedly, "My breath, my breath!" Then the awakening became complete, and with a subsidence of facial expression to the normal state my uncle seized my hand and began to relate a dream whose nucleus of significance I could only surmise with a kind of awe.

He had, he said, floated off from a very ordinary series of dream-pictures into a scene whose strangeness was related to nothing he had ever read. It was of this world, and yet not of it—a shadowy geometrical confusion in which could be seen elements of familiar things in most unfamiliar and perturbing combinations. There was a suggestion of queerly disordered pictures super-imposed one upon another; an arrangement in which the essentials of time as well as of space seemed dissolved and mixed in the most illogical fashion. In this kaleidoscopic vortex of phantasmal images were occasional snapshots, if one might use the term, of singular clearness but unaccountable heterogeneity.

Once my uncle thought he lay in a carelessly dug open pit, with a crowd of angry faces framed by straggling locks and three-cornered hats frowning down on him. Again he seemed to be in the interior of a house—an old house, apparently—but the details and inhabitants were constantly changing, and he could never be certain of the faces or the furniture, or even of the room itself, since doors and windows seemed in just as great a state of flux as the more presumably mobile objects. It was queer—damnably queer—and my uncle spoke almost sheepishly, as if half expecting not to be believed, when he declared that of the strange faces many had unmistakably borne the features of the Harris family. And all the while there was a personal sensation of choking, as if some pervasive presence had spread itself through his body and sought to possess itself of his vital processes. I shuddered at the thought of those vital processes, worn as they were by eighty-one years of continuous functioning, in conflict with unknown forces of which the youngest and strongest system might well be afraid; but in another moment reflected that dreams are only dreams, and that these uncomfortable visions could be, at most, no more than my uncle's reaction to the investigations and expectations which had lately filled our minds to the exclusion of all else.

Conversation, also, soon tended to dispel my sense of strangeness; and in time I yielded to my yawns and took my turn at slumber. My uncle seemed now very wakeful, and welcomed his period of watching even though the nightmare had aroused him far ahead of his allotted two hours. Sleep seized me quickly, and I was at once haunted with dreams of the most disturbing kind. I felt, in my visions, a cosmic and abysmal loneness; with hostility surging from all sides upon some prison where I lay confined. I seemed bound and gagged, and taunted by the echoing yells of distant multitudes who thirsted for my blood. My uncle's face came to me with less pleasant associations than in waking hours, and I recall many futile struggles and attempts to scream. It was not a pleasant sleep, and for a second I was not sorry for the echoing shriek which clove through the barriers of dream and flung me to a sharp and startled awakeness in which every actual object before my eyes stood out with more than natural clearness and reality.

V.

I had been lying with my face away from my uncle's chair, so that in this sudden flash of awakening I saw only the door to the street, the more northerly window, and the wall and floor and ceiling toward the north of the room, all photographed with morbid vividness on my brain in a light brighter than the glow of the fungi or the rays from the street outside. It was not a strong or even a fairly strong light; certainly not nearly strong enough to read an average book by. But it cast a shadow of myself and the cot on the floor, and had a yellowish, penetrating force that hinted at things more potent than luminosity. This I perceived with unhealthy sharpness despite the fact that two of my other senses were violently assailed. For on my ears rang the reverberations of that shocking scream, while my nostrils revolted at the stench which filled the place. My mind, as alert as my senses, recognised the gravely unusual; and almost automatically I leaped up and turned about to grasp the destructive instruments which we had left trained on the mouldy spot before the fireplace. As I turned, I dreaded what I was to see; for the scream had been in my uncle's voice, and I knew not against what menace I should have to defend him and myself.

Yet after all, the sight was worse than I had dreaded. There are horrors beyond horrors, and this was one of those nuclei of all dreamable hideousness which the cosmos saves to blast an accursed and unhappy few. Out of the fungus-ridden earth steamed up a vaporous corpse-light, yellow and diseased, which bubbled and lapped to a gigantic height in vague outlines half-human and half-monstrous, through which I could see the chimney and fireplace beyond. It was all eyes—wolfish and mocking—and the rugose insect-like head dissolved at the top to a thin stream of mist which curled putridly about and finally vanished up the chimney. I say that I saw this thing, but it is only in conscious retrospection that I ever definitely traced its damnable approach to form. At the time it was to me only a seething, dimly phosphorescent cloud of fungous loathsomeness, enveloping and dissolving to an abhorrent plasticity the one object to which all my attention was focussed. That object was my uncle—the venerable Elihu Whipple—who with blackening and decaying features leered and gibbered at me, and reached out dripping claws to rend me in the fury which this horror had brought.

It was a sense of routine which kept me from going mad. I had drilled myself in preparation for the crucial moment, and blind training saved me. Recognising the bubbling evil as no substance reachable by matter or material chemistry, and therefore ignoring the flame-thrower which loomed on my left, I threw on the current of the Crookes tube apparatus, and focussed toward that scene of immortal blasphemousness the strongest ether radiations which man's art can arouse from the spaces and fluids of Nature. There was a bluish haze and a frenzied sputtering, and the yellowish phosphorescence grew dimmer to my eyes. But I saw the dimness was only that of contrast, and that the waves from the machine had no effect whatever.

Then, in the midst of that daemoniac spectacle, I saw a fresh horror which brought cries to my lips and sent me fumbling and staggering toward that unlocked door to the quiet street, careless of what abnormal terrors I loosed upon the world, or what thoughts or judgments of men I brought down upon my head. In that dim blend of blue and yellow the form of my uncle had commenced a nauseous liquefaction whose essence eludes all description, and in which there played across his vanishing face such changes of identity as only madness can conceive. He was at once a devil and a multitude, a charnel-house and a pageant. Lit by the mixed and uncertain beams, that gelatinous face assumed a dozen—a score—a hundred—aspects; grinning, as it sank to the ground on a body that melted like tallow, in the caricatured likeness of legions strange and yet not strange.

I saw the features of the Harris line, masculine and feminine, adult and infantile, and other features old and young, coarse and refined, familiar and unfamiliar. For a second there flashed a degraded counterfeit of a miniature of poor mad Rhoby Harris that I had seen in the School of Design Museum, and another time I thought I caught the raw-boned image of Mercy Dexter as I recalled her from a painting in Carrington Harris's house. It was frightful beyond conception; toward the last, when a curious blend of servant and baby visages flickered close to the fungous floor where a pool of greenish grease was spreading, it seemed as though the shifting features fought against themselves, and strove to form contours like those of my uncle's kindly face. I like to think that he existed at that moment, and that he tried to bid me farewell. It seems to me I hiccoughed a farewell from my own parched throat as I lurched out into the street; a thin stream of grease following me through the door to the rain-drenched sidewalk.

The rest is shadowy and monstrous. There was no one in the soaking street, and in all the world there was no one I dared tell. I walked aimlessly south past College Hill and the Athenaeum, down Hopkins Street, and over the bridge to the business section where tall buildings seemed to guard me as modern material things guard the world from ancient and unwholesome wonder. Then grey dawn unfolded wetly from the east, silhouetting the archaic hill and its venerable steeples, and beckoning me to the place where my terrible work was still unfinished. And in the end I went, wet, hatless, and dazed in the morning light, and entered that awful door in Benefit Street which I had left ajar, and which still swung cryptically in full sight of the early householders to whom I dared not speak.

The grease was gone, for the mouldy floor was porous. And in front of the fireplace was no vestige of the giant doubled-up form in nitre. I looked at the cot, the chairs, the instruments, my neglected hat, and the yellowed straw hat of my uncle. Dazedness was uppermost, and I could scarcely recall what was dream and what was reality. Then thought trickled back, and I knew that I had witnessed things more horrible than I had dreamed. Sitting down, I tried to conjecture as nearly as sanity would let me just what had happened, and how I might end the horror, if indeed it had been real. Matter it seemed not to be, nor ether, nor anything else conceivable by mortal mind. What, then, but some exotic *emanation*; some vampirish vapour such as Exeter rustics tell of as lurking over certain churchyards? This I felt was the clue, and again I looked at the floor before the fireplace where the mould and nitre had taken strange forms. In ten minutes my mind was made up, and taking my hat I set out for home, where I bathed, ate, and gave by telephone an order for a pickaxe, a spade, a military gas-mask, and six carboys of sulphuric acid, all to be delivered the next morning at the cellar door of the shunned house in Benefit Street. After that I tried to sleep; and failing, passed the hours in reading and in the composition of inane verses to counteract my mood.

At 11 a.m. the next day I commenced digging. It was sunny weather, and I was glad of that. I was still alone, for as much as I feared the unknown horror I sought, there was more fear in the thought of telling anybody. Later I told Harris only through sheer necessity, and because he had heard odd tales from old people which disposed him ever so little toward belief. As I turned up the stinking black earth in front of the fireplace, my spade causing a viscous yellow ichor to ooze from the white fungi which it severed, I trembled at the dubious thoughts of what I might uncover. Some secrets of inner earth are not good for mankind, and this seemed to me one of them.

My hand shook perceptibly, but still I delved; after a while standing in the large hole I had made. With the deepening of the hole, which was about six feet square, the evil smell increased; and I lost all doubt of my imminent contact with the hellish thing whose emanations had cursed the house for over a century and a half. I wondered what it would look like—what its form and substance would be, and how big it might have waxed through long ages of life-sucking. At length I climbed out of the hole and dispersed the heaped-up dirt, then arranging the great carboys of acid around and near two sides, so that when necessary I might empty them all down the aperture in quick succession. After that I dumped earth only along the other two sides; working more slowly and donning my gas-mask as the smell grew. I was nearly unnerved at my proximity to a nameless thing at the bottom of a pit.

Suddenly my spade struck something softer than earth. I shuddered, and made a motion as if to climb out of the hole, which was now as deep as my neck. Then courage returned, and I scraped away more dirt in the light of the electric torch I had provided. The surface I uncovered was fishy and glassy—a kind of semi-putrid congealed jelly with suggestions of translucency. I scraped further, and saw that it had form. There was a rift where a part of the substance was folded over. The exposed area was huge and roughly cylindrical; like a mammoth soft blue-white stovepipe doubled in two, its largest part some two feet in diameter. Still more I scraped, and then abruptly I leaped out of the hole and away from the filthy thing; frantically unstopping and tilting the heavy carboys, and precipitating their corrosive contents one after another down that charnel gulf and upon the unthinkable abnormality whose titan *elbow* I had seen.

The blinding maelstrom of greenish-yellow vapour which surged tempestuously up from that hole as the floods of acid descended, will never leave my memory. All along the hill people tell of the yellow day, when virulent and horrible fumes arose from the factory waste dumped in the Providence River, but I know how mistaken they are as to the source. They tell, too, of the hideous roar which at the same time came from some disordered water-pipe or gas main underground—but again I could correct them if I dared. It was unspeakably shocking, and I do not see how I lived through it. I did faint after emptying the fourth carboy, which I had to handle after the fumes had begun to penetrate my mask; but when I recovered I saw that the hole was emitting no fresh vapours.

The two remaining carboys I emptied down without particular result, and after a time I felt it safe to shovel the earth back into the pit. It was twilight before I was done, but fear had gone out of the place. The dampness was less foetid, and all the strange fungi had withered to a kind of harmless greyish powder which blew ash-like along the floor. One of earth's nethermost terrors had perished forever; and if there be a hell, it had received at last the daemon soul of an unhallowed thing. And as I patted down the last spadeful of mould, I shed the first of the many tears with which I have paid unaffected tribute to my beloved uncle's memory.

The next spring no more pale grass and strange weeds came up in the shunned house's terraced garden, and shortly afterward Carrington Harris rented the place. It is still spectral, but its strangeness fascinates me, and I shall find mixed with my relief a queer regret when it is torn down to make way for a tawdry shop or vulgar apartment building. The barren old trees in the yard have begun to bear small, sweet apples, and last year the birds nested in their gnarled boughs.

—THE END—

HOWARD PHILLIPS LOVECRAFT (1890–1937) of
Providence, Rhode Island was a relative unknown
in his brief lifetime, maintaining a modest and
secluded existence writing short stories for pulp
magazines. Lovecraft is now recognized as a
pioneer of weird fiction, holding a place beside
Poe and King at the vanguard of American horror.

"Herbert West: Reanimator" was written over the period of
October 1921–June 1922 and serialized in the February–July 1922
issues of amateur publication *Home Brew*.

"Pickman's Model" was written in September of 1926 and
originally published in *Weird Tales* magazine's October 1927 issue.

"Cool Air" was written in March of 1926 and originally published
in the short-lived periodical *Tales of Magic and Mystery*, March
1928 issue.

"The Thing on the Doorstep" was written in August of 1933 and
originally published in the January 1937 issue of *Weird Tales*.

"The Shunned House" was written October 16–19, 1924 and
originally published twelve years later in *Weird Tales*, October 1937
issue, after Lovecraft's death in March of the same year.

More Books in the Supernatural History Series

———

The Wonders of the Invisible World
Cotton Mather

More Wonders of the Invisible World
Robert Calef

*A Report of the Mysterious Noises Heard in the House
of Mr. John D. Fox in Hydesville, Arcadia, Wayne County*
E.E. Lewis

Hydesville: The Story of the Rochester Knockings
Thomas Olman Todd

Spiritualism: The Open Door to the Unseen Universe
James Robertson

The Vampire; A Tale
John Polidori

The Were-Wolf
Clemence Housman

———

Found at foxediting.com/books/ and at online and specialty bookstores.
Supernatural History Packs available at etsy.com/shop/theotherfoxshop.